Pâtissier et Étranger

"A delightful adventure that held me enthralled from start to finish. This novella is guaranteed to bring a smile to your face, an acceleration to your pulse and a rumble to your stomach."

—Kate Heartfield, author of *The Embroidered Book*

"An unexpected blend of the bakeries and thrills, of the perils of espionage and the pleasures of a good pastry. The spy who came in from the cold wishes he picked this spot."

—John Wiswell, author of *Someone You Can Build a Nest In*

Pâtissier et Étranger

Laurence Raphael Brothers

BRIGIDS GATE PRESS
Overland Park, Kansas
www.brigidsgatepress.com
Printed in the United States of America

For my parents ... again

Chapter 1

I have loved mille-feuilles since I was a child

Paris, 1967. Cordon Blanc Institut de Cuisine et de Pâtisserie.

Madame Dulaurier stroked a white-gloved finger across the gleaming stainless-steel surface of the oven that had been assigned for my use. Finding no trace of soot or grease to complain of, our professeur turned to my work counter and inspected my recipe card. I'd filled it out with the details of the pastry I intended to bake for tomorrow's examination, which if I passed would result in the award of a diplôme de pâtisserie.

"Mille-feuilles?" She raised an arch eyebrow. "Monsieur Drake. You do realize we award no points for difficulty? A complicated pastry will be judged with the same rigor as a simple one. And pâte feuilletée requires a lot of prep time. Are you sure you wouldn't rather try madeleines instead?"

Without having to look I could tell Brigitte at the baking workstation to my left and Jean on my right were both hugely amused, though neither would dare say a word under Madame's withering gaze.

"Madame," I said, "I have loved mille-feuilles since I was a child. They are the reason I seek certification as a pâtissier from the Institut under your masterful tutelage."

To my surprise she smiled at me.

"Hmf. Flattery will get you nowhere, young man. In this instance. But very well. I suppose we must make allowances for an English eccentric.

Because of all the dough turns you'll have to go through, I assume your colleagues here have no objection to an early start tomorrow?"

"Not at all, Madame professeur," said Jean, and Brigitte said, "Of course not. And anyway, my tarte takes time, too."

"Very well. Your examination will begin tomorrow at eight. All ingredients must be presented prior to preparation."

Madame approved Jean's financiers and Brigitte's proposed tarte au chocolat without further complaints and swept out of the student kitchen like a monarch departing their audience chamber.

When our teacher had safely departed, Brigitte burst out laughing. "A close call! She almost used the Look on you."

I shuddered. "Yes. That would have been bad. I might have melted. Or evaporated entirely."

We students liked to pretend Madame had supernatural powers, but really it was her seigneurial air combined with her awesome mastery of pâtisserie. The Dulaurier Look of Disdain was something else, though. It could have been weaponized and used for crowd control.

Jean shook his black-haired Gascon head and said, "Well, as for me, I'm taking her advice with my financiers. Quick, easy, no complications, just prepare beurre noisette, stir up the batter, and bake. So long as I can get them out of the pan without sticking, I'm golden." He paused, smirked in charming fashion. "But I really have to salute you, George. By the time she's done judging your mille-feuilles, I could probably pass with burnt bricks."

I chuckled, but inwardly I wasn't so confident. I'd meant what I'd said about the mille-feuilles. Making one perfectly had been my goal since I'd started at the Institut. But only recently had my efforts come to look like anything like proper pâtisserie products instead of clumsy messes.

"I'm sure you'll do just fine," said Brigitte kindly, possibly noticing my unease. She began peeling off the regulation student smock we'd all been wearing for the pre-exam formalities, and though she was perfectly chastely dressed, I looked away regardless because, well, just because. When I looked back, she caught my eye and smiled at me, and I blushed despite myself, which made her grin even more broadly. She was a slight, sharp-featured woman with dark skin and reddish-black hair, wearing bell bottom jeans and a long jonquil tunic belted with a sash. Her uncanny golden eyes tended to catch and hold my gaze at embarrassing moments. Despite the attraction I felt, I'd resolved not to approach her because my staring was improper enough as it was, and I didn't want to make her uncomfortable sharing a kitchen with me. And anyway, I was happy just to be her friend.

She was about to say something else when the kitchen door opened again. It was the Institut receptionist. "A call came for you, Mademoiselle Lejeune," she told Brigitte, handing her a note.

"Thank you." She glanced at it. "Merde! There's no time!"

In a moment, her whole demeanor had changed from light-hearted to urgent.

I couldn't help but ask, "Brigitte, what is it? Is something wrong?"

She shook her head. "It's nothing. But … George, would you do me a very great favor?"

"Of course."

"You still have that cute little Vespa, right?"

"Yes."

"Be a dear and go to the Moulins Bourgeois. They're holding a special order for me."

"What? But isn't that—"

"Yes. In Verdelot. I'm so sorry, I know it's a terrible imposition. But I promise to make it up to you, so—please?"

"Of course," I said, "but are you in some kind of trouble, apart from that? Can I help, somehow?"

"Oh, no," she said. "Just—just a minor family emergency. Thanks so much, though! Tell them my name and the word bibelot, they'll give you the bag, it's already paid for. You'll remember, right? Bibelot?"

And like that she was gone, leaving me and Jean both bemused.

"Better you than me," he said, shaking his head. "But you should hurry if you want to beat the rush hour."

Verdelot was 50 kilometers east of Paris. I'd never visited the famous mill there, but I'd heard they had a shop that sold small specialty orders to individual bakers. Of course, the Institut had all the standard pastry flour one might ever want, but just the right mix and grind might well improve a pie crust or a choux. I'd been planning to take the rest of the day off to prepare mentally for the baking test tomorrow. This would probably be a loss of three hours even if I didn't get stuck in traffic, but I could hardly back out now.

"Ring me up when you get back," said Jean. "Geneviève has a friend she wants you to meet, and there's a bistro I've been meaning to try, too.

Afterward, we're having a little PAN-watching party on Geneviève's roof. Have you ever been to her place? It's wild!"

Geneviève was Jean's girlfriend, a student in the Institut's school of cuisine as opposed to pâtisserie. She was also close friends with Brigitte.

"Pan-watching?" I asked, wondering if it had anything to do with bread rising. "What's that?"

"Oh, sorry. What is it in English? UFO? Phénomène Aérospatial Non identifié. People have been talking about lights in the sky lately, but I haven't seen anything yet myself."

"Ah. Me neither, but I'll definitely give you a call when I get back." I put my smock in the laundry bin, shrugged on my jacket from where it had been hanging in the closet, and was on my way. Really, I was quite fond of both of my kitchen-mates, and indeed everyone at the Institut had accepted the crazy English pastry student with much greater bonhomie than I'd expected when I enrolled.

I'd just filled up my Vespa, so Verdelot and back wouldn't be a problem. It was a pleasant afternoon in late spring, a bit on the warm side, but the breeze was cool enough once I got going. I had the usual difficulty working my way out of the city, but the N3 was an easy ride this time of day. I rode past endless stretches of golden wheat fields whose harvest would no doubt be delivered to the Moulins Bourgeois. I might have been a bit uneasy about riding a moto to somewhere in the French heartland I'd never been before, but it would hardly be possible to get lost looking for one of the most famous mills in the entire country in a town only a couple of kilometers off the highway.

I stopped at a tiny brasserie in the quaint old hamlet of Viels-Maisons for a bite of ficelle picarde, a savory pancake stuffed with ham and mushrooms and topped with melted cheese. The snack gave me a chance to confirm my directions. On reaching Verdelot five minutes later, the mill proved impossible to miss. I was quite pleased with myself. It had only been an hour and a half since leaving Paris, no mishaps or wrong turns along the way. The next hurdle would be convincing them to give me Brigitte's order.

The Moulins Bourgeois consisted of a mansion-like hall across from an old brick tower with an odd house-like structure perched atop it, surrounded by modern industrial buildings where no doubt all the milling now took place. I pulled into a large parking lot dominated by heavy lorries all bearing the mill logo and walked into the lobby of the main building.

A friendly receptionist directed me to the shop, which was next to a display of antique mill machinery. There wasn't much to it; a smallish room with a sales counter, walls covered with commercial posters featuring scantily clad models posing with large sacks of wheat, and an easel displaying a list of prices for various grades of flour in two- and five-kilo quantities. No one was present, so I tapped the bell on the counter and a moment later a heavyset man with a dark five o'clock shadow appeared from a back room. He wore a green workman's jumpsuit, and as he approached the counter he was brushing crumbs off his lapel.

"Sorry for interrupting your meal," I said.

"No problem."

"I'm here to pick up a package for Brigitte Lejeune. She said it was already paid for."

"Lejeune? I don't know. I'll have to check."

He disappeared again. I waited a full five minutes, growing more and more impatient, wondering if I was going to have to return to Paris empty-handed. I resolved to buy a few kilos of different kinds of pastry flour just in case she could make use of it.

At last, a different man arrived, this one tall, thin, and balding, with a narrow black mustache. He was wearing a business suit. Definitely not a clerk or a workman. Possibly a manager.

"I'm sorry," he said. "Monsieur—?"

"Drake. I'm here to pick up Brigitte Lejeune's order. Oh! She said to tell you 'bibelot'. I hope that's right."

He switched to English, which annoyed me, because I thought my accent was undetectable. But apparently not quite. "Ah. Just so. She called to let us know. Would you identify yourself, please, sir?"

"Huh? I suppose." I took my carte de séjour out of my wallet. "Will this do?"

He studied it with what I thought was insulting care and copied down the number into a little notebook.

"Just so. Please wait another moment."

The man vanished into the back room, and returned with a two-kilogram sack. He handed it over with a grunt, having scattered some loose flour on his otherwise pristine suit jacket. This couldn't be his regular job. I looked at the label. It seemed like a standard mill product, something you might find at any grocery, except—

"This is type 55. Are you sure that's right?"

"What?" He seemed bemused. "Type what?"

"Type 55. Flour for baguettes. But Brigitte is a pastry chef. She must have asked for type 45. Would you check again, please?"

The man was taken aback, but he rallied strongly. "Sir, I assure you this is Mademoiselle Lejeune's parcel. I am quite certain."

Though I was sure they'd screwed up Brigitte's order, I could hardly dispute him further. "Oh, very well. But, say, would you throw in two kilos of type 45, farine de gruau? And another two of type 45 farine de blé? I'll pay for them, of course."

He looked like he wanted to protest, which seemed a bit odd, but after an awkward moment, he turned and called "Jules! Jules! To the front, please."

Jules reappeared. I repeated my order, paid the man, hefted the additional two sacks into my cradled arms, and walked out. Mission accomplished, more or less. I was still a bit puzzled about what had just happened, and worried that Brigitte wouldn't be happy with her order. But really, regular pastry flour should be perfectly fine for a tarte au chocolat in which the ganache was the star performer.

Chapter 2

He was shooting at me

I put the sacks into the panniers of my Vespa, Brigitte's type 55 on the left side and the two I'd purchased on the right. I'd just gotten into the saddle when I heard a deep-throated engine rumble and a shiny black Citroën DS pulled out of the lot. That manager was the driver. He must have been in quite a hurry, as I hadn't wasted any time before returning to my moto. And indeed, he burned rubber blasting his way down the narrow lane back to the highway. Oh well; perhaps he also had a date in Paris he didn't want to miss.

At first the ride back to the city was as pleasant as the way out had been, but then I ran into a traffic jam on the N3 just past Meaux. I would have gone around the line of stopped cars on my Vespa, but there were flashing lights ahead from the Gendarmerie and I didn't dare. It took half an hour before they set up a lane for traffic on our side of the road to pass. And then I saw it: a cluster of identical unmarked cars cordoning off the wreck of a black Citroën DS. The front end was somewhat crumpled, but it didn't look like a lethal accident. The cars must have come from some branch of the Sûreté, who normally wouldn't turn out for a highway accident as such things were the gendarmes' responsibility.

I was certain it was the manager's car from the mill, and I had to admit it gave me pause. The combination of his curious behavior, the oddity of Brigitte's order, the man's haste in driving away, and now this unusual security service presence for an ordinary car wreck. What could it mean?

I couldn't imagine intrigue being associated with an order of flour for a pâtisserie examination, but still it was, well … intriguing.

By the time I got past the jam, the sun was close to the horizon, which was annoying because I was heading west and it was in my eyes. Maybe it was because I was shifting my gaze around to avoid the glare that I picked up a motorcycle closing from behind in my mirror. I glanced over my shoulder to see a big new Norton Commando roaring towards me. Reducing my speed a little, I pulled over to the side of the road to admire the machine and let it pass. The rider was hunched over in an uncomfortable position and he didn't overtake me but instead slowed down to match my speed. Suddenly my side-mirror shattered. For a moment I was more annoyed than anything else—I'd paid good money for that mirror, as the scooter hadn't come with one—but then I realized what was happening. The motorcycle rider was bracing a pistol on his handlebar, and he was shooting at me.

The shock of the realization was almost fatal because the rider's second shot smacked into my scooter's frame, fortunately not hitting either me or anything crucial in the drivetrain. Then I unfroze, swerved to the side before a third shot could hit me, but realized there wasn't much I could do to get away. My Vespa's speedometer topped out at 100 kph, but I doubted it would even go that fast, whereas the big Norton could probably do twice that.

I swerved again; another shot, another miss, and I noticed a white plume had begun to flow from the back of my scooter like it was an old biplane trailing smoke from an oil fire. One of the bullets must have pierced my pannier and flour was streaming out behind me. I was hoping it wasn't Brigitte's special order when the idea struck me. I knew even as I was thinking it how reckless it was, but I was out of options. I braked as hard as I could without losing control and for a moment the white cloud was in the motorcyclist's helmeted face. I'm sure he could have just ignored the cloud, but he swerved to avoid it anyway. By then it was too late for him to slow down. He had to pass me if he didn't want a collision. It was just luck that I guessed wrong which side he was going to pass me on, and just luck that my own swerve hit him at precisely the right point for him to lose traction and spin out. I really should have crashed myself, but though the impact sent me into the oncoming traffic lane, fortunately there wasn't anything there. I just managed to make it back over to my side without falling over or hitting anything.

I didn't stick around to see what happened to the motorcycle rider, but there were no more shots, anyway. The pannier was no longer trailing a plume of flour, but I wasn't inclined to stop and check the bags, either; for quite a while I was too shaken up to do anything more than just keep riding.

After the shock wore off, the question was what to do next. First I thought I should turn around and go back to the wreck site to find a gendarme or a Sûreté officer to report the attack. But the motorcyclist might be back on his bike and still looking for me. And also, I figured that the city was my best bet to get out of harm's way. I turned off the highway to take smaller roads back to Paris. I spent the rest of the ride swiveling my head looking for the Norton coming up behind me and trying to figure out how and why I'd been attacked in the first place. But I couldn't come up with any explanation that made much sense.

I was torn between seeking refuge at the British embassy near the Champs Élysées, going to the Quai des Orfèvres to report the attack to police headquarters, to Rue des Saussaies for the Sûreté, or finding Brigitte to get some answers. I didn't know where she lived, though, and I didn't have her number, so that was out, at least for today. Dealing with Parisian traffic took all my attention when I reentered the city. I must have unconsciously adopted my usual approach of hoping that my problems would just go away on their own, because I didn't go to any of the destinations I had in mind but found myself instead heading home. It didn't even occur to me to be cautious in approaching my block of flats on the outskirts of Montparnasse. I deliberately didn't look my Vespa over for damage as I propped it up and chained it in the alley next to my building, because I knew the bullet-hole in the pannier would only make me sick to see it.

It was only as I was actually entering the old building, a shabby prewar whose tiny elevator was always broken, that I realized I might be doing something stupid. But the concierge, Madame Bernard, who'd held the post for the last fifty years, told me no strangers had even entered the building that day. I felt it was safe enough to go upstairs. I rented the top-floor flat at a discount because of all the stairs. It was a bit late for prudence, but I tried to unlock my door as quietly as possible and tiptoed around without turning on any lights until I was satisfied no one was lying in wait for me. Then I picked up the phone and called Jean.

"George? Good timing! You're still going out with us?"

"I am. But do you happen to know Brigitte's number?"

"No, sorry. I think Geneviève does, though, so you can ask her. We're meeting at the bistro Deux Verres just off the Rue de Grenelle at eight. You know how to get there?"

"I'll find it."

The sun was still technically up when I left my flat, but it was invisible behind the bulk of the city's buildings. I felt a little better prepared to confront reality now, so when I entered the alley, I popped open the damaged pannier of my Vespa to see what had happened to Brigitte's order.

Within I found a half-full sack of flour laying on its side, the top torn open by a bullet. I hefted the torn sack to put it inside another larger bag I'd brought down with me, and I felt a hard object under my fingers within the partially empty pouch. It turned out to be a polished gray ovoid, featureless and smooth, eight centimeters long. Basically egg-shaped. The thing was unusually warm to the touch with a faint iridescent sheen to the material like an oil slick or a soap bubble. I wasn't sure if it was stone or metal.

Just like that I felt sick at heart again, the capsule's strangeness forcing me to relive the whole attack. And doing that made me realize the incredible luck involved in my escape, and how close I'd come to getting killed.

I'd like to say I had some rational thoughts about the object, but I was so creeped out I almost threw it away. I had my arm poised, even, and it was only fear that I might get Brigitte in some kind of trouble that held me back. I didn't want to carry the capsule around with me, not for any rational reason but because I had the crazy feeling it might draw more assassins or whatever that motorcyclist was. The narrow alley where I parked my moto had an old bricked up doorway midway along its length, and there was just enough of a lintel that I could put the thing up on the lip of the bricks out of sight of anyone walking by.

I felt a lot better after getting rid of the mysterious capsule. Getting back on my Vespa, I set off for the Deux Verres with Brigitte's half-full sack now inside a brown paper bag. Not that the remaining baguette flour was going to be of any use to her, if Geneviève could help me track her down tonight, but it felt like the thing to do.

The bistro proved to be an old-fashioned place on a side street near the Hotel des Invalides. I parked my moto at the curb just by the door, the spot a lucky find in this neighborhood. A bunch of older regulars were drinking at the zinc-topped bar when I entered, and a few people were dining, but all the tables near the bar were doubles, none occupied by my friends. After asking a waiter working out front, I found Jean and Geneviève at a quad in the back room, which was otherwise unoccupied.

Geneviève looked up as I entered. She was a tall brunette who spoke with a refined, elegant diction, always wearing suits by Chanel, today's being a black and white ensemble that suggested a sailor's garb. She and Jean had been together for a while now, and I knew she was Brigitte's friend too, but I had only met her in passing a few times and didn't know her well. She waved me over, and Jean looked up to see me.

"Hey, George. Glad you made it!"

He was going to say something else, but I interrupted.

"Listen, you'll never believe what happened to me, but I really need Brigitte's number. It's urgent. Do you have it, Geneviève?"

"Why yes," she said, "but there's no need."

"What?"

"She's our fourth tonight. Here she is, now, in fact—Merde alors! Brigitte!"

I turned to look, and there she was, looking terribly bedraggled, draped in an oversized windbreaker, standing unsteadily by the dining room's back door. She held a pistol in her left hand, and her right was stiff at her side. As I watched, frozen momentarily in shock, a drop of blood fell from her fingertip to the floor.

"Hello, George," she said. "I'm sorry for the trouble but—"

She paused, shuddered and swayed, and that gave me just enough time to leap forward and catch her before she collapsed. I wound up sitting on the floor with Brigitte in my arms. I wanted to find out if she was seriously injured, because that drop of blood seemed like a bad thing, but I was afraid to do anything but just hold her.

Chapter 3

State security and counterintelligence

Geneviève quickly picked up Brigitte's pistol from where it had fallen. She fiddled with it, maybe making it safe, and put it into her handbag. Jean hesitated, clearly not knowing what to do. After a moment he asked, "Should—Is she okay? Should I call an ambulance?"

"Not yet," said Geneviève. "Let me take a look at her first."

I was relieved that Geneviève felt competent to deal with this situation, because I certainly wasn't. She knelt beside us, took Brigitte's pulse, then rolled up Brigitte's sleeve to reveal an ugly gash below her right shoulder. The wound was five centimeters long and almost a centimeter in width. It looked like it had bled quite a bit judging from the stains on her arm and sleeve, but now no blood was flowing at all, which seemed a bit odd for such a large gouge.

"Hm. Shock, I suppose," said Geneviève. "She probably just fainted. If she doesn't come out of it—"

Brigitte stirred in my arms. She stiffened, her eyes fluttered open, and she tried to sit up, so I helped her, and we wound up sitting side by side on the floor, me still supporting her torso, just in case.

"George?" her voice was urgent. "George, did you—did you get my order?"

"It's safe," I said. "You're safe. You fainted. You'll be fine."

"It's not here?"

I was conscious of Geneviève and Jean close by. It wasn't that I didn't trust them, but I didn't want to get them any more involved in Brigitte's trouble than they had to be. Not with mysterious assassins wandering around loose. So, I decided to be circumspect even though I wanted to pump her for information.

"No," I told her. "I left it behind. But I can get it whenever you like."

"Merde! Is there—is there a sweet I can have? Candy, a pastry, anything."

"What?" I wasn't sure I'd understood what she said. Jean appeared equally bemused, but Geneviève was more decisive.

"They must have desserts here," said Geneviève. "Hang on. I'll get something from the bar." She strode through the door into the front room.

As soon as she left, Brigitte whispered to me, speaking fast. "George, there's an item in the sack of flour."

"Yes, I found it accidentally."

"Listen, I might faint again. If I do, if I don't wake up, you have to stop me from being taken away in an ambulance. Just get the thing, put it in my hand. All right?"

"Yes, but—"

"But you want me to explain. I will, I promise, it's just—ah, damn …"

Brigitte sagged against me, her head flopping down to rest on her shoulder. Out. I could see she was breathing deeply, but I was worried there was something wrong with her beyond just the wound and shock. Unfortunately, I couldn't do anything for her apart from laying her down on the floor as gently as I could, using my jacket to make a pillow for her head. She seemed to be sleeping, but of course that couldn't be true.

Jean asked, "What's she talking about? And what's with the gun? Do you think that could have been a bullet wound? A graze? Do you know what's going on, George?"

"Not even a little. But it's something weird. I almost got killed on the way here."

"What?"

"Someone on a motorcycle was shooting at me on the N3 on the way back from Verdelot. It was only luck that I escaped."

"You'll have to tell us everything." That was Geneviève, returning with a plate of éclairs and a pitcher of ice water. "Wait, Brigitte—did she faint again?"

"Yes. But I'm afraid it's something more than that."

Geneviève looked her over again. "A faint wouldn't last this long. I'd almost say it was hypoglycemia. But that's impossible."

I shook my head. "She's always eaten our pastries with no problem, right Jean?"

"Oh yes," he said. "And her own. Definitely a sweet tooth. No way she's got diabetes. She may possibly have skipped lunch, but we had breakfast together, and she ate pain au chocolat, not to mention an omelette with bacon."

"Listen," I said, "she told me to get something, I think it's something that will help her. But she doesn't want to go to hospital. Geneviève—"

"No hospital," she said decisively. "Not unless she takes a turn for the worse. Help me to prop her up in a chair. Jean, tell the waiter she's drunk and sleeping it off if he asks. Okay?"

"But what if—"

"Just do it," said Geneviève. The hints of commanding authority she'd shown in the last couple of minutes, an aspect of her personality I hadn't seen before, were doubled and redoubled in her voice now, and I didn't blame Jean for meekly obeying. Together we got her seated in a chair at our table, and indeed she looked like she might have had too much to drink.

"You'll have to take care of her for a few minutes," said Geneviève. "I need to make a call. George, walk with me."

"But—" Jean tried to get a word in, but Geneviève cut him off.

"Five minutes," she said. "Don't worry." She took my arm and walked me out through the back door before I could come up with anything to say myself.

We emerged in an enclosed court, the backs of several buildings facing onto it, a narrow lane connecting out to some side street.

"There's a phone in the bistro front room," I said. "No need to find one on the street."

She shook her head impatiently. "This is no time for dicking around. I'm DST. Are you with Station P?"

"Station P?"

"SIS. MI-6. They call their Paris office Station P."

"What? What?" Finally her meaning got through to me. MI-6. The Secret Intelligence Service. "No, I'm not! And I don't even know what DST is!"

"You're kidding me. Direction de la Surveillance du Territoire. Police nationale. State security and counterintelligence. And if you're not with MI-6, then—"

"I swear! I'm not with anyone. I'm just a student pâtissier. That's all I am!"

"Fuck. I hate all this compartmentalization. Listen to me, George, listen carefully."

"I'm listening," I said.

"Brigitte's my friend, but it also happens to be my job to protect her without her knowing it. If you're from MI-6, you're supposed to be on the same side as me, but if you are, you'd be breaking the agreement, same as me, right?"

"Agreement? I have no idea what you're talking about," I said. "But I do want to help Brigitte. That's why I went out to Verdelot today, to get the flour she wanted from the mill."

"The flour. Right. You got it from a DST agent. Who was run off the road ten minutes after he gave it to you. He's in hospital now with a concussion. And you escaped the DCRG man who got him too. Come on, now. Who are you with?"

"What's—"

"Another Sûreté department. Police intelligence, such as it is."

"You're fighting your own people? But that doesn't make any sense!"

"Came as a surprise to us, too, you know? Someone must have turned. Probably it's just a few double agents, but everything has been chaos since the afternoon, and the situation is … fluid. But don't change the subject. I can arrest you and throw away the key if I want to. So, give it up. Who are you with?"

"I swear," I said, "On my honor, I'm just a student chef. When I get my diplôme de pâtisserie, I'm going home to Cambridge to open a shop. I don't know who Brigitte really is, or what's going on. Maybe that's why she asked me to get the flour for her."

"You escaped from a professional hit-man on the open road. He's in hospital now, too, with a broken pelvis, and he admitted who he worked for. He was after you because of what you got from M. Monier at the mill, and you disposed of him without even using a gun."

"It was just luck that I got away!"

I told her what happened, and Geneviève shook her head. "You're either the world's worst secret agent or the world's luckiest pastry chef. For the sake of argument, say I believe you. You've got her package? From the mill?"

"Yes. I'll bring it back here. Should be under an hour."

She sighed. "All this secrecy, I don't even know what's in the package. But Brigitte likes you. You know that's why she showed up here tonight? It wasn't chance. She asked me to invite you, to make a fourth for our little party, because she wanted to meet you outside the kitchen. She said you were shy. So, she gets into some kind of jam, she probably got shot, and she still came here, not even knowing who I really work for. She came for you."

"Wow. I had no idea. This—well it doesn't change anything I was going to do. But—"

Geneviève laughed. "Sure. So go get her package. Be careful. I'd call in backup to escort you, but all the agents with clearance are committed elsewhere now that those DCRG salauds are on the other side. I'm not even allowed to talk to regular Sûreté people who haven't been cleared for this. And I need to stay here in case someone else comes for Brigitte. Jean is sweet, but I'm sure he's no operative, anyway."

"Okay. Thanks for trusting me."

"Who said I trust you?" But she patted me on the shoulder as she turned back to the bistro. "It's Brigitte who trusts you. Good luck."

I walked around the block to get back to my Vespa, seeing assassins lurking in every shadow. Maybe because she was sure I was some kind of agent I hadn't told Geneviève how freaked out I was to be in this situation. And maybe I'd thought it was cool to seem like one to her, but now I was having second thoughts. If the DCRG knew enough to ambush me on the highway, why wouldn't they be able to find out who I was and where I lived? For a few minutes on the way back to Montparnasse I was scheming how to convince some random person off the street to retrieve Brigitte's capsule and get it back to me unobserved. But if there was anyone watching the area around my home they'd have infinitely more experience with that kind of thing than I did and all I'd be doing was putting some other person into danger. At last, I decided to do it on my own, and I had one little idea how to make it at least a bit safer.

Rather than heading straight for my block of flats, I parked the moto a hundred meters away. There was a café across the street from the alley in which I'd left the capsule, and I figured if I got a table there and watched for a few minutes, I ought to be able to see anyone on the street who was hanging around. I sat down near the front and ordered a cone of frites and a beer, because I hadn't eaten anything since that pancake back in Viels-Maisons and dinner looked like it was being delayed. I didn't see anyone loitering in the street, and the part of the alley I could see was deserted too. If it weren't for my fries I'd have probably gone straight for the capsule, but they came out of the kitchen smelling so good I couldn't bear not to eat a few. Even with mayonnaise and no vinegar they were divine, ambrosial in what had been an astonishing and wearying day. So, I gave my stomach five minutes, and that's why I noticed the guy sitting alone at the patio table pretending not to be studying the scene across the street.

I'd just about convinced myself I'd been safely anonymous, but looking him over from behind and to his right, I couldn't imagine anyone more obviously an agent of some kind. He was big and brawny, wearing a blue wool suit in the warm weather, and when he raised his arm to take a sip of his drink, I saw the fabric bulging around what had to be a holster.

I froze in my seat for a minute, unable to think or act, despite the fact he clearly had no idea I was there. The spell of panic was broken when a waitress asked me if I wanted anything else. I'd visited this café a few times before, it being so close to my flat, and so I recognized her though I didn't know her name. The idea came to me like that, the same way as that idiot notion with the flour stream, and I just ran with it.

"That guy over there," I spoke as quietly as I could and still be heard in the noisy café room.

"Yeah? What about him?"

"He's an investigator," I lied, "a divorce investigator."

"Ugh," she said. "What a pig!"

"There's a certain young woman in my building. I want to warn her … but he's watching. You don't suppose … you could accidentally spill some water on him or something? I just need a minute to get by him."

Even as I said it, I knew how crazy it sounded, and how full of holes. But my luck was in. Maybe the waitress had reason to resent someone like that guy, or maybe she just trusted me. The fifty-franc note I put down on the table to cover my ten-franc tab might have helped, too.

"I can do it," she said, smirking. "Just watch!"

It was really a beautiful sight. She stopped the waiters' station and returned with a full carafe of ice water. Just as she passed the man's table, her foot skidded out from under her somehow, and while losing her balance and falling down, her arm swung back and hit him in the crotch with the carafe, ice-cubes and water splashing all over him. Just the impact alone made me wince. The man convulsed out of his chair and wound up on the floor. He choked off some expletive that sounded like "blyad" to me, but must have been something else, garbled.

Now was the time. I rushed by the man, crossed the street against traffic, darted into the alley, grabbed the strange capsule from the bricked-up lintel, shoved it in a pocket, and returned to the street again. My heart was racing but I forced myself to walk casually, mingling with the other nighttime pedestrians till I made it around the corner to where my Vespa was parked. No one shot at me, no one called out, and I couldn't see anyone pursuing me either.

The ride back to the bistro was even more fraught and anxious for me than the ride out, but I encountered no difficulties, and made it to the Deux Verres in time for my estimate.

"But what if he doesn't—" Jean spun around as he heard me enter. "Oh! George! You're back!"

Chapter 4

An excellent meal in plain style

Nothing much had changed in the bistro back room since I left. Brigitte was still zonked out in a chair, Geneviève sitting beside her. Jean across from them. A bottle of wine was on the table along with a plate of gougères and another of escargots. A waiter must have come and gone a few times, presumably buying the idea that Brigitte was just sleeping it off.

"You have what she wanted?" Geneviève asked.

"Yes. A bit of an adventure along the way, though." I was pleased with how casual my voice sounded.

"I see. Nothing immediately dangerous to Brigitte, though? You weren't followed?"

"I don't think so."

"Good. Now, Jean, I'm sorry, but I'd like you to leave the room for a few minutes."

"What? Why?"

"It's for your own good," she said. "You're already in enough danger, my dear. I just don't want to expose you to anything more than you've already taken upon yourself."

"But I don't understand at all. It doesn't seem fair, either. I mean, George is going to stay, right?"

Geneviève sighed. "I won't insist. I've got far too little support just now. It's just—well, this is going to be an absolute top state secret, I expect. I'm not really just a secretary in the Sûreté … actually I'm a security officer. If you stay, the DST is going to turn you over, look into your past, bother your family, your friends, unearth your every secret. There will be oaths to take, documents to sign, it will be a huge hassle. But if I testify you weren't exposed to confidential information—"

"I see you've been keeping things from me." said Jean, slowly. "But you really think I'm going to back out now? After this build-up? If you wanted me gone you should have sent me on an errand like George."

She reached out and put her hand over his. I thought his answering blush was rather charming.

"More than one secret, I'm afraid. But no doubt you're right. I have to admit, really I wanted you to stay. On your head be it, but thank you, dear." She turned to me. "George? You want to complete your errand? What was it, some special flour or something?"

"Not exactly." I took the strange little capsule out of my pocket. "This was hidden in the package I got from the mill. I suppose it was your fellow officer, the one who was run off the road, who arranged it."

"Yes. I didn't have a need to know, myself, not till now. Poor Monier. He's not a field officer at all. Just an analyst. But we have so few people in the Brigitte compartment, and it must have seemed like a safe enough assignment. I'm just happy he wasn't seriously injured."

The Brigitte compartment? Of course, I had a million questions saved up over the course of the day, and some of them Geneviève might even have answered. But they could wait another minute, anyway. I walked over to Brigitte's chair, raised her limp arm and put the capsule in her hand, wrapping her fingers around it like I was giving a rattle to a baby.

Honestly, I don't know what I was expecting. On the one hand, the gesture could hardly be expected to do anything for her at all, but on the other she *had* asked me to do it, and the thing was clearly something extraordinary seeing as secret agents were going to such trouble to obtain it.

For a moment, I felt a tingling in my fingers where they were in contact with the egg now in Brigitte's hand, like pins-and-needles, but deeper, somehow. I moved my hand away cautiously in case it looked like Brigitte was about to drop the thing, and the sensation faded. A few seconds passed with nothing more happening, and then her eyes opened.

She smiled. "George! You got it! Thank you so much!"

Geneviève asked, "Are you all right?"

"Totally," said Brigitte. She got up from her chair and executed a pirouette. "See?"

She nodded to Geneviève. "But it seems you've been rather naughty, Gigi, keeping secrets from me like that."

Geneviève was taken aback. "What? You knew?"

"I'm teasing you. You had me completely fooled until just now. But I sort of came and went a few times over the last few minutes, and I overheard a bit. Now I know you're not just a student chef. You're a kind of nanny for me, aren't you? But you're my friend, too, and so I forgive you. And I'm so sorry about your colleague, M. Monier. It's my fault for putting him in danger."

"Thank you," said Geneviève after another pause.

Brigitte said, "I'm sure you'd all like some kind of explanation. I bet even Gigi has some questions she'd like answered. So why don't we finish our dinner here, then we can go looking for PANs and I'll reveal everything. I have a sort of intuition we'll see something up there too, you know?"

"But—"

"I'm supposed to keep it all secret? Yes, and you people aren't supposed to follow me around with spies and keepers, no matter how charming. Anyway, George and Jean are also my friends, and between the two of us, we've gotten them mixed up in my affairs. They deserve to know everything, too. And don't forget, I'm graduating the Institut if I pass my exam tomorrow. I won't be your problem after that."

"I'm worried about the danger you're in," said Geneviève stiffly, avoiding Brigitte's eyes, "not just about keeping everything secret. You got shot earlier, and you still haven't said what happened. And what with the attacks on George and M. Monier … The truce has been broken. There are probably agents from any number of foreign intelligence services converging on Paris right this second."

Brigitte patted Geneviève's hand, and the DST officer blushed. It occurred to me Brigitte had a talent for causing this reaction. "You're very sweet, and really, that was quite a close call for me earlier today. I should have been more careful. But now, well …" She held up the capsule. "I have nothing to fear."

And like that, the egg vanished. It couldn't have been sleight of hand, she hadn't moved at all, it was just that the thing was gone now. Geneviève blinked, opened her mouth, then closed it without saying anything. I had the feeling she was astonished but didn't want to show it. I exchanged a glance with Jean and he shrugged as if to say he had no idea either. Then

I looked again. Was it possible that the iridescent sheen I'd seen on the surface of the capsule was just barely visible on Brigitte's hand? As I stared it faded away.

"Right then," said Brigitte. "Jean, this place was your idea, wasn't it? What's on the menu?"

Jean had a choice, to ask what had just happened or to ignore it, and he made it for all three of us. "Ah … I heard their choucroute garnie is especially good. Also, their pot-au-feu with sauce pauvre-homme."

It was a struggle at first not to speak about the obvious things, but Brigitte was the soul of conviviality, talking about food, about baking and the history of pâtisserie, about tomorrow's exam, about Geneviève's own course of study in the school of cuisine, and whether she had anyone like our dauntless Madame Dulaurier as an instructor. All three of us were a bit stiff to begin with, but one by one we broke down and submitted to our hostess's obvious desire to speak only of everyday things. Though coming to this place might have been Jean's idea originally, and though Geneviève might have assumed a domineering attitude as a DST officer earlier, it was Brigitte's party, now. And by the time we'd finished the hors d'oeuvres and a bottle of the bistro's surprisingly good vin de table, we were all relaxed and chatting freely as if nothing untoward had taken place that day. To be honest, this was what I wanted too, to put it all behind me and pretend no one had ever shot at me, and also to pretend that there were no unresolved mysteries hanging over us.

It was an excellent meal in plain style, satisfying my ideal of a perfect night out: delicious food eaten in company with good friends. But at last, we finished with our oeufs à la neige, which Brigitte was particularly pleased with, licking the last drop of crème à l'anglaise from her finger like a greedy cat. Now it was time to go, and quite possibly I'd have my fragile pretense of normality shattered yet again.

Geneviève had a flat not far off the Rue de Grenelle in the area between Gros-Caillou and Les Invalides, a moderate walk from the bistro Deux Verres. I was imagining a subdivided apartment in one of the old Haussmann-era tenements. While most of the city still conformed to the baron's architectural rules, the original buildings had often been allowed to slide into genteel seed. But her place was splendid, not just spic-and-span but kept in exquisite shape, from the gleaming brass window grills to the polished marble floors of the atrium to the antique elevator with its gilt metal cage door. Even the concierge was extraordinary, not the usual pensioner but a beautiful young woman dressed in the latest Dior oblique pattern who paid the sort of refined respect to Geneviève that you might expect from a lady in waiting.

"Wow," I said, as we rode the elevator, "the Sûreté must pay a lot more than I would have guessed." I was immediately ashamed of myself, not only for the vulgarity but because we'd been so good about not talking about intrigue and danger for the last two hours.

Geneviève colored, and I was ashamed again for mentioning it, but Jean spoke up eagerly. "She's Fézensac nobility! Last scion of a Montesquiou cadet branch, which since I'm from Artagnan makes us almost cousins in a way. Adds spice … if you know what I mean."

She laughed; I couldn't see due to the way we were all standing pressed together in the tiny elevator, but I think she must have goosed Jean or performed some other intimate maneuver, because he gave a little start and abruptly flushed red himself. But she'd regained her composure, which I expect was the point of his intervention.

"In fact," she said, "My family once owned the whole building, but now all I have is the garden and the penthouse. No étage noble for me! And I'm afraid my pay, which isn't nearly as grand as you might think, goes mainly into keeping the place up and paying its taxes. So, while I did put aside a bottle of calvados for our little party, you mustn't expect VSOP."

We stopped at Geneviève's flat on our way up to her rooftop garden. The apartment featured three bedrooms (one with a boudoir, one converted to a library), and included a formal dining room, an extensive kitchen with breakfast table, a drawing room, and an enormous salon. All the rooms except the kitchen (which was fully modernized) were ornately furnished with what had to be authentic Empire antiques.

"It's like living in a museum," she said. "I hardly dare to touch anything outside the kitchen. The only other room I really live in is my bedroom. But I have to admit, the rooftop garden is a real benefit of the place. I rent it out for parades and holidays and that almost pays for the cleaning people."

In addition to the calvados, she'd laid in port, sherry, and Vichy water, not to mention a tray of pistachio and raspberry macarons. "Store-bought," she said, "I wouldn't dare compete with the experts." We carried them all up a wrought-iron spiral staircase to a turreted landing that opened out onto the promised rooftop garden. The garden proved to be a lovely little thing, five meters by eight, its tiled floor surrounded by planters and troughs overflowing with flowers. In the center of the space, a long bronze-framed table was topped with mottled sea-glass. Since there were no taller buildings close by, we had a grand view of the left bank ranging from the illuminated Eiffel Tower and the expanse of the Champ de Mars on the one hand to the baroque dome of the St. Louis Cathedral des Invalides on the other, while the Seine was a dark snake to the north lined with illumination on its various quays.

It was a clear, cool night, and a gentle breeze stirred the air, but due to the skyglow from the City of Lights, only a few of the brightest stars were visible. Geneviève made sure we each had what we wanted to drink and we dutifully ate a macaron apiece—really, they were quite good—but this was just preparation for whatever Brigitte had to tell us. She stood up at the head of the table and raised her snifter, and we all quieted down.

Chapter 5

A vast vortex of light

B efore I begin," she said, "I'd like to thank you all. My three best and only friends in all the world." She raised her glass. Jean and I followed suit, but Geneviève hesitated.

"You realize I was assigned to you? That we didn't meet by accident?"

Brigitte smiled warmly at her. "So you're not really my friend at all? You've just been obeying orders and playing a part? Do you honestly expect me to believe that, Gigi?"

"Ah … well. I didn't say I'm not fond of you …"

"And I am fond of you too, Gigi. Very much so. And deeply grateful for your friendship. So. To your very good health!"

We drank up and then Brigitte said, "Right. Here we go. This is a PAN-watching party, right? People have reported lights in the sky lately, I understand."

"Yes," said Geneviève. "Just like two years ago. When—"

"When I started at the Institut."

"Hey," said Jean. "Wait a minute …"

Brigitte raised her hand in the air and made a fist. Her hand began to glow with a yellow-white light that slowly shifted towards an actinic blue. From over the horizon in all directions, a dozen dots of light appeared, growing larger as they came closer. Their cores were white and iridescent halos played around them. At first their motion appeared almost random, darting around like excited hummingbirds, but they gradually approached us, assuming a spiral pattern, converging on us at the center of a vast vortex of light and—

She lowered her hand, the light faded, and the glowing bodies hesitated, seemingly disappointed, and then, one by one they streaked away in random directions until all trace of them had vanished. The display took less than a minute from start to finish. We were all speechless, spellbound the whole time.

"Okay," said Brigitte. "Let's see now. Where is it? Oh, yes." She produced an index card. "I made some notes."

She took a deep breath.

"I'm from a planet in a distant solar system. We call it Blossom. We're pretty sure our ancestors were transported from Earth to our world, probably around five hundred thousand years ago. No plants or insects produce sugar on Blossom, which is why I'm studying pâtisserie here. Our science is only a few decades more advanced than yours. But we've had sparklets—those flying lights—in our world since before our history began. We've only just now learned how to use them for transportation. We suspect they were introduced by the same beings who transported us to Blossom, but there's no way we can be sure."

I think we were all too stunned to respond to that, on top of the light display. At least I was, anyway.

"Let's see," said Brigitte. "What else? Oh, that egg thing is a sparklet controller. We're not even close to understanding how it works, but every group of twelve sparklets somehow creates one of these eggs. Whoever has the egg can summon the whole swarm for transportation. By themselves, the sparklets only breed very slowly. But it turns out if you subject the controller to intense radiation, they breed quite a bit faster. That's where my own controller has been for the last couple of years, in your nuclear reactor core at Chinon. The deal we made with your five permanent security council governments is to give each country their own sparklet, which in due time will breed more, until eventually you have twelve of your own. Perhaps it will only be twenty or thirty years. Or perhaps you'll have to wait until you have five groups of twelve if your governments don't share them."

Geneviève was the first of us to recover.

"I … wow. I guess there's a higher compartmental clearance than the one I've got. I knew there was something special about you, but …" Geneviève shook her head. "I really had no idea about any of this."

Brigitte smiled. "I was required to keep it all secret myself, as part of the agreement. But the agreement also said I'd be left alone and not monitored by your security services. And since that seems to have been breached since day one, well … The good part of that is now I feel free to tell everything to my friends."

"And the bad part is … you got shot? What happened this afternoon?"

"Ah … Well, this is a little embarrassing. I'd like to say we're superior to you poor benighted Earthlings with all your little countries and all your horrible wars. But we have other kinds of conflict."

"She's beating around the bush," said Jean in a stage whisper. It seemed he'd recovered from his own surprise at Brigitte's revelations. "It really must be embarrassing."

"Yes. It's a bit involved, too. There's one big biological difference between our peoples. We regenerate from wounds very quickly. It just takes a lot of bodily energy. Mitochondria, right? Other animals in our world can't do it, so this too might have been a gift from the people who planted us on Blossom. It's good and bad. Because if we're seriously injured, we tend to pass out if we don't have enough glucose available in our blood."

"Oh!" Geneviève was quicker on the uptake than Jean and me. "So, this afternoon, when you fainted—"

"Exactly. Actually, I'd been shot twice, once through the torso. I was on my last legs when I made it to the Deux Verres."

"That's why you wanted a sweet at such an odd moment."

"Yes. Though it was probably too late to do me much good at that point. But see, that's another benefit of the controller. It powers the owner's, what do you call it? The Krebs cycle? That's why I said I had nothing to fear anymore when you brought it back to me, George."

I finally had something to say. "So really, pâtisserie is doubly important for you to learn. Not just because your people have never tasted the glory of the French dessert, but for health reasons as well."

"Yes! We lose too many people every year to regenerated injuries because they go into hypoglycemic shock if it takes too long to get them to a hospital. I'm bringing back fruit tree seeds and sugarcane cuttings when I return home. We can synthesize sugar in the laboratory, of course, or process starch for it, but it's expensive and not available in our groceries. Not part of our culture. Most of our people have never eaten anything sweet at all."

Honestly, I wanted to forget about everything else, all about the spy stuff, even about the sparklets, and just talk about how much fun it would be to introduce pâtisserie to an entire world of people who'd never tried it before. But Geneviève wasn't so easily put off.

"Okay," she said. "This is all marvelous and fascinating, and honestly I can hardly take it all in. But you haven't told us what happened to you this afternoon. Who shot you, and why did they do it?"

Brigitte didn't say anything for a moment. She bowed her head, and took a deep breath before answering. "You understand these things better than I do. Let me just give the facts, then you can tell me if my suspicions are correct."

"We only have a few flocks of sparklets in our world. And yours is the first planet we've traveled to since we discovered it was possible. I've been on my own since I arrived here three years ago. But we'd already learned something about Earth through, ah, covert visits. In case anyone from my world needed to reach me in an emergency, we set up an answering service and recognition signals and a rendezvous. That way they could contact me quickly from any phone booth, and we could meet if necessary"

"You don't have any … futuristic communications devices you could have used?"

"Ha," said Brigitte. "We sure do. You'll have them too in a few years when you come up with better batteries and more compact electronics. But the portable phones we use rely on having a wireless network available. Using native tech seemed easier.

"Anyhow, the controller at your reactor finally generated a new sparklet. It was all arranged for me to take it back today. But then I got that message from my service, and it had the recognition signal. I couldn't meet my compatriot and retrieve the controller at the same time, so I sent George to your poor M. Monier who'd been overseeing charging it up at the reactor. He was the one to come up with that elaborate charade at the mill. I had no reason to expect the errand would be dangerous. I'm so sorry about that, George!"

The me of six hours ago might not have agreed, not while being shot at on the N3, but the current me had survived, and was very pleased with the opportunity to be gallant.

So, I said, "Absolutely not your fault. It was urgent, you needed it done, and it might have saved you too. Honestly, I'm delighted to have been of service."

"Thank you for being so kind! But I know I'm in your debt. Anyway, after I sent you off on that errand, I went to the rendezvous and this man, an Earthling I'm sure, showed up and shot me. Twice, once in the chest.

Didn't say a word. He was a little surprised when I didn't fall down, and even more when I plucked the gun out of his hand; that's when I got the arm wound. Then he ran away. I knew I didn't have much time before regeneration shock hit me, so I went to Deux Verres where we were supposed to meet up, hoping that George had the controller."

"What a terrible time that must have been," said Geneviève. "But that recognition signal disturbs me. I assume you didn't tell it to anyone?"

"No."

"I'm afraid you must have an enemy back home. Maybe someone colluded with one of the foreign spy services, who activated their own resources in the DCRG to try and grab your controller when they thought M. Monier or George here had it. Do you know anyone who might want to harm you? Anyone with access to ... to your travel technology?"

Brigitte bit her lip. "I ... it's complicated. I want to think of, of ... I could call them the Templar faction. I want to think of them as just opposition. Not as enemies. But you're right. There's no other explanation. Fortunately, this whole thing should blow over on its own."

"What? Why?"

"I was planning to remain here for a while after graduation. But if I go home right away, I'll be taking my controller and the sparklets with me, and there won't be anything left for anyone to fight over. No doubt my people will send someone else back here eventually. But the main thing is I don't want to endanger you or George or Jean."

"I don't mean to be snide," said Geneviève, "but it's a bit late for that. All of you had better stay overnight in my flat here. Perhaps this fiasco with the DCRG will have been resolved by tomorrow morning and I can get some backup."

We finished our drinks on a somber note, and Geneviève led us downstairs. There was a cabinet in the dining room that I would have supposed held table settings or glassware, but Geneviève unlocked it to reveal a rack of firearms.

"Do any of you shoot?" She took a lethal-looking military rifle out of the case. "FN FAL. I also have a Mossberg 500, an Ingram M10, and a Browning Hi-Power, if you prefer."

"I went through my service year like everyone else," said Jean. "But to be honest, much as I'd like to show off for you, Gigi, I'd rather not carry a weapon. I wasn't a good shot in training, and I'm afraid I might be more dangerous to us with a gun than to any attacker."

"And I've never even fired a gun," I told her. "I don't think any of these would be much use to me."

"Entirely optional," said Geneviève. "I really doubt we'll be attacked; no one on the other side should know Brigitte is here, or even that I'm a DST officer. But the guns are here if the need arises. They're all loaded, and I'm not locking the case tonight."

She took the automatic rifle with her, however.

"Now then," she said, leading us into the hall. "Brigitte, this will be your room. The linens were just changed, and there's clean nightgowns and a bathrobe in the wardrobe. George, Jean, you can share a bed in the other bedroom if you don't mind."

"Not at all," said Jean after glancing at me and receiving a nod in return. "But what about you, Gigi?"

"I shall be awake, in a chair, outside Brigitte's door. I let her out of my sight on her own for one afternoon and she got shot. There will be no repeat."

"In that case," he said, "I'll stay up with you."

"No. You have your examination tomorrow. You'll need your sleep. Same for you, George."

"But you're having your own exam, too! A whole meal, right?"

"I'm not the one who's really going to become a chef," said Geneviève. "Going to school is just a cover for me. Anyway, I can make consommé and Bourguignon in my sleep."

"I … oh, all right. But I need a word with you first, if you don't mind? It's … rather important to me."

Jean and Geneviève stepped off into another room for their conversation. What I wanted now was a heart to heart with Brigitte. And no one was stopping me from approaching her, either. No one but myself. I was thinking, come on, you can't tell a space alien that you find her attractive. You can't even tell her you want to be her friend. Because—it will seem like—I couldn't even explain it to myself. I just knew I couldn't do it. If only today had been a normal day. If only there had been no revelations, no one trying to kill me … but I had to wonder even then, even though it seemed Brigitte had arranged the night just to spend some time with me, if I'd have been brave enough to talk to her.

Chapter 6

A curious mix of emotions

On entering our Institut kitchen the next morning along with Jean, I felt a curious mix of emotions. I should have been keyed up to a state of extreme tension because I couldn't afford another year of classes and the diplôme de pâtisserie symbolized a necessary hurdle for moving on with my life.

Today, though, all that seemed unimportant. What was important to me was—what? Exactly, what? My involvement with Brigitte was going to bring me to the attention of not just the DST but also MI-5, not to mention whichever ministry committees were in on the secret back home. Probably be an interesting few weeks, to say the least. But that wasn't it, either. They'd discover I really was just a baker, my parents a postman and an NHS doctor respectively, and they'd realize it was totally impossible that I might be a foreign agent, not even a French one.

So, I had to sneak up on my understanding of what I was feeling. Enlightenment came as I wondered what Brigitte was doing. Geneviève was arranging some kind of covert means of transporting her to the Institut this morning. Both Jean and I had wanted to accompany them, but she'd said it wouldn't be as easy with more people. I was worrying about where Brigitte was, whether they'd gotten into trouble with enemy spies or with Sûreté double agents and hoping she wouldn't be late, because more than anything I wanted her to try my mille-feuilles and tell me she liked them.

"Don't worry," said Jean, putting on his smock. "They'll be here."

And like that, I understood. What I wanted wasn't Brigitte as a lover. Well, okay, actually maybe I did, but that was secondary. More importantly, I wanted her as a friend. I wanted what we had now. And I understood how much I didn't want her to go. Because she would likely never return, or if she did, it would probably be years and years and what were the odds she'd even look me up?

"Pardon me, messieurs. I am here to clean up."

I almost didn't turn around. We students had to keep our ovens, stoves, and utensils immaculate, but janitors would stop by to empty bins from time to time. After a moment of stupidity, though, I recognized the voice.

"Brigitte!"

"It's me." She was dressed in a drab jumpsuit and workman's cap, carrying a bucket and mop. "Geneviève is outside, she said something about a security sweep."

"A security sweep for a baking examination."

"For a space alien's baking examination, perhaps it makes more sense?" Brigitte curtsied. "But you know, despite everything, I find I am eager to begin. Let's set out our ingredients. It won't be long before Madame makes her entrance."

I turned to the pantry and then the refrigerator, making sure everything was ready. This wasn't the time or the place to talk to her about my feelings, not with everything hanging over us. I set out everything I needed except the butter, which had to remain in the refrigerator to prevent it melting into the pâte feuilletée later on, and the marble rolling pin which likewise had to be chilled. Laying everything out was calming, and by the time I had the ingredients ready, all my bowls and pans and whisks and everything lined up neatly, I was as eager as Brigitte to start baking.

"I was wondering," said Jean, abruptly. "What's it like?"

Brigitte turned to look at him. "What's what like?"

"Traveling with those sparklet things."

"Oh! It's the best! It's a mind-blowing experience. See, when you summon them, like I halfway did last night, they surround you and merge together like a big suit made of light. You can see these … these links connecting your world to others. Like strands of a spiderweb. And you can look down them, too, sort of move your point of view around and zoom in on things like a, a movie camera. That's how we knew coming here wouldn't strand us in deep space or on a world with no air. We spent a long time spying on your world before coming ourselves, trying to learn the language from analyzing billboards and watching people's mouths moving and like that. Anyway, when you travel across a link, it's like flying through a tunnel of stars, a passage of light. … you go faster and faster, and there comes a moment … I have no words for it. Just glory, is all. Having experienced it, I could almost believe what the Templars say, that the gods themselves gave us the sparklets. In fact—"

"In fact, it sounds like an Explorer is having second thoughts about her rejection of the true faith."

I turned to see a chalky-skinned man had just entered the kitchen. He was dressed in a fawn-colored trench coat and a black beret. The crew-cut hair that showed beneath his cap was silver, but not the shade of graying hair, nor even that of an ash blond, but something closer to actual metallic silver. His accent was thicker than Brigitte's, but otherwise clearly similar.

"Trenco!" She raised her hand, prompting the man to mirror her gesture.

"Birgud." He nodded to her. He started speaking in a language I didn't recognize, then glanced at Jean and me, and switched back to his heavily accented French. "You have nothing to fear from me. As you see, the controllers cancel one another out. I can't use mine as a weapon against you even if I wanted to. But I *can* prevent you from returning to Blossom to contaminate our people still further."

"Brigitte," said Jean. "Is this … person troubling you? Because we can take care of him for you if he is." He glanced at me and I nodded back at him.

"Ah, yes," said Trenco. "Typical homo sapiens response. Aggression, right from the outset. Wise men, do you call yourselves? Should be homo malus, don't you think?"

"Salaud! Don't you flaunt your pacifism at me, Trenco," said Brigitte. Her gaze was so intense that I expected the man to spontaneously combust. "Your agent shot me in the chest yesterday. You put one of the people guarding me in hospital, and you almost killed my friend!"

To my vast surprise, Trenco sank to his knees and bowed his head.

"I'm sorry," he said. "I know that's a feeble thing to say, but I do apologize. I was taken in by the people I was working with. They assured me they wouldn't use violence. But I've broken with them now. It seems I was naïve. Too naïve for this hellish world."

"Hellish?" I asked. "Is it really that bad, Brigitte?" I couldn't help butting in.

She shook her head. "Not at all. It's an article of their faith, you see. They believe many things that aren't supported by facts."

Trenco regained his feet.

"Earth is a world of iniquity and sin, overtaken by … by demons. The Lords of Light rescued us, the Chosen, and transported us to a world free from the influence of the Twisted Ones. And now, having stolen the divine sparks once under our loving protection, you Explorers want to defile us with the vile fruits of this corrupt world. Do you wonder at our opposition?"

Brigitte (Birgud?) sniffed. "And do you wonder that the Templars have been a dwindling minority for over two hundred years now? So diminished that after thousands of years of custodianship, they were finally forced to yield a pod of their precious sparklets to people who knew and appreciated what they could do."

"Hmph." Trenco seemed disdainful. "Well, in any event, you won't be bringing any disgusting native foodstuffs back with you. Our controllers cancel each other out. I can keep you here on this … Earth … indefinitely."

Perhaps it hadn't occurred to Trenco that force might be applied to him, too. But on the one hand I thought his naïveté made him rather a better kind of enemy than most, and on the other I didn't want to look like a demon to him so I didn't point it out. Jean seemed piqued, however.

"So, you really intend to do what, live here with us on this hell-planet for decades to keep Brigitte from returning home? Does that really seem like an act of virtue to you? Is it even practical?"

Trenco shuddered. "If necessary. I hope to convince Birgud of her error in good time. I should be delighted to return home with her if she pledges to bring nothing back. But I expect this dreadful world will convince her soon enough if my own arguments fail. Look at the allies I found here, just to begin with. They swore to me they'd support my righteous cause, and then they betrayed me almost at once. What horrors will you people reveal to her next?"

Brigitte said, "It seems we're at a bit of a stand for now. I suppose the good news is that I'll have to stay on a bit longer. But this business with foreign spies and double agents … it may have been Trenco's foolishness that provoked it, but I hate to think I'm putting you in continued danger."

All of us were silent for a moment. Since I couldn't think of anything better to do or say, I turned back to my ingredients and my utensils, readying everything for the examination. That's when it occurred to me.

"Pardon me, Monsieur Trenco," I said. "You've just come to our world recently? You haven't had time to acclimate yourself?"

"That's right," he said. "I learned French while I was at home, in preparation for the divine transit. Your languages are a popular course of study, you see, a fad among our people. Another corrupt transmission from this horrible world, but I suppose it proved useful."

"Do you understand why we're here? Do you even know what this place is?"

"What?" Trenco considered the question. "Is this ... some sort of refectory kitchen?"

"No. This is a training institute for pâtisserie. You Blossom people have never eaten anything like it. But we students will be devoting our lives to preparing just this kind of food. It's a joy and a solace for millions of people around the world. There are pâtisseries in every country on Earth."

"But—"

"And this is our final examination. We'll be baking the best pastry we possibly can, to be judged by our teacher. It's a very important day for all of us, including Brigitte. That's how she's spent her time on Earth, learning to bake alongside us. But here you are, a newly-arrived visitor, arrogantly claiming you know what's good and evil in our world without even having experienced any of it for yourself. And you have the audacity to cite the violence you yourself provoked as evidence of our sins! If you hadn't come here, it wouldn't have happened."

"I ... there is some justice in what you say. And yet I can't permit your corrupt crafts to be transmitted to Blossom. The scripture is very clear—"

"Listen," said Jean. "Why don't you just sit down and watch us bake. When we're done, you can sample our work and decide for yourself if it's good or evil."

Brigitte was delighted by the idea. "Yes! Is it not written, 'by their presents their virtue shall be known'? Come, Starborne, you must at least give us a trial before you make up your mind."

Trenco bowed his head. "Very well," he said. "I owe you that much consideration. If I can't resist whatever foul lure this food of yours has to offer, there's no sense in standing in the way of your return. I accept your challenge."

A moment later, Madame Dulaurier and Geneviève entered, in conversation.

"Really, Mademoiselle de Fézensac," said our professeur, "with all respect, I can't imagine anyone would attack the Institut. The very idea is ludicrous. But if such a contemptible thing *were* to occur, I suppose we would have to shrug and accept our fate. We have nothing like a security force, not even a pensioner on guard duty. Indeed, that is what the Sûreté is for, is it not? To relieve our minds of such concerns?"

Geneviève grimaced. "Touché."

It was pleasing to see the changes her expression ran through as successively: her face lit up to see the three of us, she registered alarm at seeing the stranger Trenco, and then she realized that he was odd enough in appearance to possibly be one of Brigitte's countrymen despite their different colorations.

Madame Dulaurier's "Mademoiselle. Messieurs." came at the same moment as Geneviève's "Who is this?"

"I'll explain," said Brigitte, taking Geneviève by the arm and whispering privately in her ear.

Madame Dulaurier said, "A guest? Acceptable, so long as he doesn't participate in the preparation or baking in any way, not even to offer advice."

"Of that you can rest assured," said Trenco. "I know nothing about … what do you call it? pâtisserie?"

Madame Dulaurier was taken aback that someone didn't know what pâtisserie was, then perhaps feeling she was being mocked, she unleashed the Look. Even not having any relation to her target I was appalled. Trenco was unable to hold out against it for more than a second; he bowed his head and muttered, "I beg your pardon," and at last Madame turned away from him as a lost cause.

Meanwhile over in the corner where Brigitte and Geneviève had retreated, the DST officer was growing more and more heated and her words became audible throughout the room. "Are you completely insane?"

"Perhaps," said Brigitte, more loudly now herself. "But I believe that he's my opponent, not my foe. And I'd rather have him as a friend. It *is* my call, in the end, isn't it?"

"Bah," said Geneviève. "I suppose. On your head be it."

"Attention, please," said Madame Dulaurier in a certain tone of voice, and we all turned to face her.

"I shall be circulating from kitchen to kitchen throughout the day to review the progress of every student being examined. When your final achievements are ready, I shall evaluate them myself. So, I'll take my leave for now. However, it appears that your group will require my *special* attention. Please don't disappoint me. Now then: you may begin."

She turned to leave, but paused. "Mademoiselle de Fézensac, I believe your own examination in the school of cuisine will soon commence. You won't want to be late. Quickly, now!"

Geneviève let out a sigh after Madame departed. "Under the circumstances it would be reckless to leave you on your own. I'll wait here. Just in case."

"Please, Gigi," said Brigitte. "I'd hate for you to miss your chance. Whatever you say, I know you've been working hard on your cuisine training. Besides, can't you check up on me while your Bourguignon is in the oven? We'll be here all day waiting for George to finish his pâte feuilletée anyway, so you can hang out with us after you're graded, too."

"I ... oh, very well. But you—" She turned and pointed a finger at Trenco who retreated a step. "If you want to find out what a demon is *really* like, you let her so much as break a nail today. You understand me?"

"Y-yes."

Chapter 7

729 layers

Of several crucial steps in making mille-feuilles, one of the most problematic for me was coming up with a clean pâte feuilletée. Tradition demanded 729 layers derived from six three-level folds. During baking, the butter in the interlarded layers would boil, releasing steam and puffing the layers apart. But that would only work properly if the butter layer was consistent, and only if it was kept cool enough not to melt into the dough.

Our first half hour was conducted in collegial silence, broken by the clink of our utensils, the shshing noises of whisks, and the whirring of egg beaters. Each of us was starting with some kind of batter, Jean making nut-cake for his financiers, Brigitte preparing pâte sablée for her tarte au chocolat, while I was stirring up my puff pastry base.

Trenco watched impassively at first, but he couldn't help but ask, "What are those ... round things?"

"What?"

"With the yellow insides."

So, we had to explain about eggs. He was horrified at first, but somewhat mollified to be told they weren't fertilized.

"Nothing lays eggs on Blossom?" I asked.

"Nothing as big as a ... a hen. But then, none of our higher animals are edible. The domesticated ones are pets and work-animals. We mainly eat vegetables and ... insects? Yes. Insects. And things ... I don't know the word. Like insects that live in the sea."

"Ah. We have those too. Lobsters and prawns and such. And various kinds of mollusks, not to mention fish."

Trenco laughed. "On Blossom the fish are more likely to eat us than the other way around. But we're poisonous to them, so they mostly don't … except by mistake."

I was coming up on my first dough turn, and I wanted to concentrate, so I apologized and asked him to wait a minute while I did it. He silenced himself and looked on with interest, almost like an anthropologist invited to some religious rite.

I spread thin slabs of cold butter on the chilled dough I'd just prepared, and rolled it out with my cold marble pin. Not bad. At least I didn't see anything that needed immediate repairs. I squared it off, folded the dough without smooshing it so far as I could tell, rolled it into shape again, and slid it all back into the refrigerator along with the rolling pin. Three layers to begin with, the dough folded like a letter being fit into an envelope.

Both Jean and Brigitte had to let their own mixtures chill for a while before baking, in Brigitte's case a couple of hours for her tarte crust, so I didn't feel too bad about the three hours of prep time required for my six dough turns. Normally we might have left the kitchen for a while, taken a stroll or passed the time at a cafe or a bistro, but we were all conscious of the unusual circumstances, and so we remained in the kitchen.

The natural awkwardness between Brigitte and Trenco was a bit of a problem early on. But Trenco was willing to answer some questions about Blossom cuisine when asked directly. It turned out that bread was a staple on Blossom, the most popular form being an unleavened savory flatbread topped with a sharp root vegetable like our garlic and the local equivalent of fried crickets (apparently they had no yeast on Blossom and it had never occurred to anyone to use chemicals for leavening). It was a favorite of both our alien visitors, with endless minor variations whose merits could be argued about. Rather like fougasse, I thought, except for the bugs. I asked about pizza; they had no cheese on Blossom due to not having any dairy livestock, which I thought almost as tragic as their lack of sweets. But they did have a wide range of tofu-like substances that served much the same purpose as cheese, and so there was an entire class of flatbread variations similar to pizza to which both Brigitte and Trenco were addicted back home.

I thought the discussion of alien cuisine fascinating, but after a while Trenco realized that he had become enthusiastically prolix about the regional varieties he favored and had forgotten he was being overly cordial to an opponent, not to mention to two possibly demonic inhabitants of an evil world. He silenced himself abruptly. By then it was time for another turn for me, and Jean's mix of wheat-, almond-, and hazelnut-flour batter was ready to pour into his financier tin. Nine layers of puff pastry dough for me, now.

Madame Dulaurier ducked in to check up on us. She gave Trenco the eye, sending some color into his pale cheeks and making him look away, noted that the financiers had just been put into the oven, and ducked out again. Time passed. Another dough turn: 27 layers.

Next it was Geneviève's turn to visit.

"Beef is cooking," she said. "I'll have to go back in a while to sauté the mushrooms. How are things here?"

"Nothing untoward," said Brigitte. "I'm waiting for my dough to set. Jean's financiers are already in the oven. In fact—yes, you can just begin to smell them now. What do you think, Starborne?"

I sniffed, and yes, I could definitely detect the aroma. The mixture of wheat and nut flour, the sugar, the almost-burnt butter, really it was as delicate and delightful as anything you might ever scent during baking.

Trenco had obviously never smelled anything like it, and it showed on his face, though he tried to suppress his reaction. Baking bread was a wonderful aroma in itself, of course, but it lacked the sweetness of cake. I guessed that a circuit that had been dormant for hundreds of thousands of years of descent in Blossom's people was activating for the first time in Trenco's head, and he wasn't sure what to make of the effect.

Ten minutes later: time for another dough turn. 81 layers.

"I always want to open the oven early to check on whatever it is," said Jean. "And usually it won't do any harm, either, it's just—"

"You're superstitious," I said. "Like me. The recipe says fifteen to seventeen minutes. You're allowed to check at fifteen, but fourteen is right out. So even if the oven might be too hot—which it isn't, rest easy—you can't check until the recipe says it's ready."

"Precisely. And the reason I bring this up—"

"You've been checking your wristwatch every thirty seconds since you put them in the oven. By my count—"

"Fourteen and forty-five seconds. Fifty ..."

Brigitte and I counted down the last ten seconds, and Jean opened his oven. A waft of aroma poured out, far richer and more intense than before.

"Oh!" Brigitte was peering over his shoulder. "They're beautiful!"

Jean put on a pair of potholder-mittens and slid his tray of tins out of the oven.

"What do you think, George? I like my financiers on the light side, but—"

"Perfect," I said, and they were.

He put the tray down on his countertop, revealing tins containing pale golden bars with smooth, almost shiny tops looking quite like bullion, the source of their name. "One tin plain, one tin with roasted almond flakes on top, one with confiture de framboise as a filling, and one I'm going to ice with a drizzle of vanilla frosting once it cools down a little."

"This is the hardest part," I told Trenco, who was trying not to look interested in Jean's baking. "The aroma is the most intense just out of the oven, but of course you have to wait for it to cool down. The ones with confiture are the most dangerous, of course."

"Dangerous?" Trenco was eager to inquire.

"Relatively speaking," I said. "You might burn your tongue on the hot jam if you don't have the willpower to wait."

"I'll put some tea on," said Brigitte, while Jean was busy preparing his vanilla icing.

Madame Dulaurier returned just at the moment when the financiers were at the point of perfection, still warm and fresh from the oven but no longer too hot to eat or decorate. Jean finished squeezing out his last artistic swirl of icing and presented the results for her judgment. She first scrutinized each pastry carefully, from all sides, including the bottom. "This one was a bit sticky," she said, pointing to a tiny patch, just a few millimeters across, where some of the cake at the base of the financier had adhered to the tin.

"Uh, yes," said Jean, a bit of sweat giving his forehead a nice sheen. "I think the one with the confiture might have been a touch too moist."

"Exactly," she said. "Which is why you oughtn't bake filled and unfilled pastries in the same batch. Now then."

She produced a small knife, little more than a scalpel really, and shaved off a paper-thin segment from the plain financier. She sniffed it, nibbled the tiniest bite, frowned and passed on to the confiture bar. This she cut down the middle, inspected the quantity of jam, made sure it wasn't leaking out of the pastry and tasted no more than the tiniest fleck of filling. She turned the almond-topped bar upside-down and tapped it to see if any of the nuts fell off, and from the frosted financier peeled off a fleck of icing to taste, no more than a few milligrams. Then she wiped her little knife off on a rag, and from her bag produced a small notebook and pencil. We were all silent while she jotted a few notes, and then she put everything away.

"Tea, madame?" Brigitte had arranged a pot and the fixings on a small tray with several cups.

"No thank you, dear," said the professeur. "But can you imagine? In classroom number three they combined to produce an exquisite presentation of a dozen kinds of petit-fours, but neglected to make an offer of tea or even café au lait. I was forced to mark them off. But very well. I shall return for the tarte au chocolat."

"Very well?" Jean exploded with the question as soon as Madame Dulaurier left. "*Very well?* What does that mean?"

"It must mean you passed," said Brigitte.

"How can you be so sure?"

"Well, first of all, she may be rather … forceful at times, but she's not cruel. And secondly, your financiers look exquisite. Let's share them out."

We split the four pastries up into five slices apiece, and Brigitte poured tea for us, explaining the choices to Trenco, who chose to take his black. I had mine black as well, Jean took lemon, and Brigitte and Geneviève both took milk and sugar, with Brigitte stirring in enough cubes to transform her tea into syrup.

"Now, Starborne," said Brigitte, "You should probably start with a bite of the plain; it's only mildly sweet."

Trenco screwed up his face in a grimace that mixed apprehension and disapproval as he tentatively conveyed a tiny forkful of the plain financier into his mouth. He seemed prepared to spit it out, but chewed and swallowed instead.

"Oh," he said involuntarily, before cutting himself off. Our alien visitor squeezed his lips into a determined frown, but it was hard to take the expression all that seriously. He took a bite of the almond-topped cake with no further reaction. Then he tried the icing-topped financier, which evidently was a grave shock, as he followed it with a sip of tea, and then … another bite. It must have been the first truly sweet thing he'd ever tasted, those few milligrams of icing. The jam, though, that was the thing. You could see his reaction plainly on his face, shock, something almost like horror, and then the realization that the intense flavor he was experiencing was actually good.

"Hundreds of millions of people here eat something like that confiture every day," said Brigitte. "Spread on toasted bread, filling a pastry, other ways, too. The glycemic load can be dangerous to some people here, and too much of it is bad for you over time, but for us it can prevent regeneration shock."

"I see."

Trenco put his fork down and took another sip of tea. I could tell he really wanted another bite of the jam-filled financier but was suppressing the urge. Geneviève made the tiniest sound, not even a snort, but she kept her face solemn. "I'd better check up on my Bourguignon," she said. "But I should be back in time for the tarte."

Shortly after the DST agent departed, Brigitte decided her pâte sablée had cooled long enough; she removed the dough from the refrigerator and formed it using a pie tin, squaring off the edges with professional deftness. She placed a blind-baking form in the interior, filled it with lentils to keep the crust from deforming while baking, and slid the assembly into the oven to bake. As she started on the filling, melting butter and cream together in a pan, the time came for another of my dough turns: 243 layers.

"Now *this*," said Brigitte, "is the true heart and soul of Earthly desserts. You'll get the aroma in a moment. There's nothing like it on Blossom, not even close."

A powerful scent arose from her mixing bowl as she poured hot butter and heavy cream over chopped fragments of dark, bittersweet chocolate.

"The essential flavor is quite bitter. But it picks up and multiplies even a hint of sweetness with enormous potency. People here eat it plain, make a drink out of it, and of course it's used in all kinds of pastries. The tarte I'm making is really not sweet at all, not compared to the jam in that financier or to George's mille-feuilles. But it's what I want to eat every day for the rest of my life. So, if you keep me here in Paris, I'll be sad for what our people are missing out on, but personally … well. I'd be overjoyed."

It didn't take long before her filling was fully combined, the scent of the hot ganache filling the room to the point it seemed like you could take a bite out of the air. Trenco tried to sit there stolidly, but it was pretty clear the aroma was tantalizing him at least as much as the rest of us.

Brigitte removed her half-baked pie crust from the oven, let it cool a bit, and then filled it carefully with hot ganache and slid the tray back into the top rack.

"This is the best part of baking," she said, showing Trenco her mixing bowl. "The leftover ganache. A perquisite of the chef." She scraped up some with a wooden spoon. "Would you like to try it?"

"I ... is this permitted? It feels wrong, somehow."

Brigitte laughed. "It's supposed to! In kitchens worldwide at this very moment, little children are hoping to be given a spoonful, and their mothers are pretending it's forbidden for just a minute before giving in. But of course, it will be better after baking in the completed tarte if you'd rather wait."

"In that case I will decline."

Brigitte licked her spoon with such a pure expression of joy on her face I could hardly bear to watch, and after a moment Trenco too looked away from her.

Her tarte was almost ready when my final dough turn came due. For once, I saw no need to perform emergency surgery on the dough. 729 layers, and I slid my pâte feuilletée onto the rack into the fridge for its final cooling cycle.

But now the tarte au chocolat was done baking, with Madame Dulaurier returning at the ideal moment to inspect the work, still hot out of the oven. She carefully considered the crust and the ganache, sniffing the aroma and bending low over the tin to look at the surface.

"Hm," she said noncommittally. Then our professeur turned to Jean. "M'sieu Periz. Someone left a message for you at the office."

"Oh?" Our friend looked a bit apprehensive. "Who was it?"

"They didn't leave a name. Just the message. Call your uncle."

"Oh ... bother. I suppose I'll have to. Please excuse me. I'll be back shortly if it's not an emergency."

Madame and Jean departed together. Brigitte slid the tin into the refrigerator to cool; as she closed the door Trenco opened his mouth. He didn't speak, but from the expression on his face it was obvious what he wanted to say; he'd supposed the tarte would be ready soon after being removed from the oven like the financiers, and now he was forlornly regretting passing up the leftover ganache. We had all skipped lunch and a few bites of financier was hardly enough. She smiled at him. "It's served chilled, you know. You'll have to wait a while."

At last, I was done with dough turns, and it was finally time for baking. The pâte feuilletée still looked good despite all the opportunities I'd had to screw it up along the way. While it was in the oven I needed to prepare my crème pâtissière filling along with some vanilla and chocolate icing, but I was feeling a bit more confident now after hours of agonizing over the dough.

At this point Geneviève returned, wheeling a cart bearing covered dishes from which the rich fragrance of bourguignon arose to do battle with Brigitte's ganache. "Nothing sweet here," she told Trenco, "just a stew with sautéed potatoes on the side. I thought you all might be eager for something more substantial than pâtisserie."

I'd been so focused on my own baking that I hadn't realized how hungry I was, but we all fell on her offering like ravenous wolves. "Where's Jean?" asked Geneviève as she ladled out the stew.

"Had to step out to make a call," I said. "Something about his uncle?"

"But he's an orphan," said Geneviève, frowning. "I suppose it's not impossible he has an uncle, nevertheless. Is all going well here?"

"Yes. His financieres were all but perfect, and I'm sure Brigitte's tarte will be as well. Even my feuilletée looks good so far. But what about you? Have you been graded yet?"

"Oh, yes." Geneviève smiled. "I passed, not that it makes any difference."

"Gigi! That's wonderful!" Brigitte hugged her. "I shall be shocked, shocked if you don't frame your diplôme de cuisine and hang it in a place of honor."

"Hm. Perhaps I will."

We passed the time until my puff pastry was done.

"Well," asked Geneviève, "how is it?"

I pulled the tin out of the oven. "Oh! It's perfect!" said Brigitte. I didn't see any flaws myself that couldn't be easily repaired when I cut the layers into rectangles to build my mille-feuilles. I set the tin aside to cool, and by then, the tarte au chocolat had finally finished chilling. This time I made sure the tea was ready for Madame Dulaurier while Brigitte concerned herself with the delicate operation of plating the tarte without damaging the crust or smearing ganache on anything.

"All right," she said. "This will be the real test, Starborne. We still have to wait for Madame to return, but after she judges my tarte, it will be your turn."

"Very well."

I had to admit, up to this minute I'd been imagining that it would be my mille-feuilles that would convince him of the essential rightness of pâtisserie. But logically it should be Brigitte's creation that posed the real test. Of course, there was nothing stopping Trenco from lying about his reaction to the tarte even if he found it as perfectly innocent and delightful as any Earthling with a love of chocolate would do. But I had the idea that he was taking the trial seriously.

The next five minutes were agony for all of us, really, gazing at the exquisite beauty of Brigitte's tarte and having to breathe in its fragrance. But at last Madame arrived. I offered her tea, which she accepted this time, taking lemon only.

"Hm," she said. "This is a basic tarte. No toppings or other embellishments?"

"No, Madame," said Brigitte. "I'm still trying to perfect the balance of flavor in the ganache. And honestly, while I have no objection to raspberry syrup or whipped cream, to please my own taste I just want to focus on the chocolate."

"Indeed." Madame Dulaurier focused her frowning gaze on Brigitte for a moment and then smiled. "I quite agree. Let's see what you've managed to achieve, then, shall we?"

We shared out wedges of tarte, poured tea for those who wanted it. And at last, I took a very small forkful. The depth and power of the underlying chocolate flavor almost made me cry, it was that moving. And the mouth-feel of the ganache and the pâte sablée crust ... exquisite.

It could be that I was predisposed to appreciate it. But all my life I'd preferred ultra-sweet milk chocolate to the bittersweet darks more common in pâtisserie and other non-candy confections. This was an eye-opening experience for me. Speaking of eyes, I saw that Trenco's were closed, the fork still in his hand as he came to grips with his first-ever taste of chocolate.

"I shall return for the mille-feuilles," said Madame Dulaurier after making a few notes in her little book.

As soon as she left, Geneviève said, "Brigitte, this is superb. It's almost ... profound."

"Yes," I said. "That's it exactly. Profound. It's truly a wonderful tarte."

Brigitte curtsied. "Thank you so much! You have no idea how much your good opinion means to me."

Trenco said nothing. I think we all wanted to know his reaction, but I didn't want to put him on the spot by asking, or even looking directly at him. Still, I couldn't help at least glancing his way, and I saw that he'd already taken a second forkful.

"I'm sorry Jean isn't here," said Brigitte. "But I suppose he'll be back soon. I'll just set aside a slice for him."

Geneviève frowned but said nothing. Something seemed to be troubling her.

Over the next few minutes, I completed my filling and toppings. The icing needed to be kept warm so it wouldn't congeal, but the crème pâtissière had to be cooled to prevent it running. Now it was finally time to assemble my mille-feuilles.

It was possible to make a single giant mille-feuille, spreading the filling on instead of piping it and then carefully cutting to make individual pastries. This was probably sensible for commercial production, but the pressure of the knife while cutting tended to smoosh out the filling unevenly, and for a fancy pastry like a mille-feuille, well, presentation wasn't everything, but it counted quite a bit. So, using a small rectangular form I'd prepared, I cut the pastry layer in advance to make twelve pieces, each eight centimeters by twelve. By then the pastry had cooled enough for me to pipe on the crème pâtissière, carefully place the middle sandwich layer, apply more crème and top it with another layer of pastry. I assembled four mille-feuilles and shaved off the errant crème with a knife. Next I piped on a smooth layer of vanilla icing to the top surface, followed by a painstaking fretwork of chocolate glacé. And then the whole tray went back in the fridge to cool.

"Well done," said Brigitte. "Such care and precision! But it looks gorgeous. I can hardly wait!"

I let out a breath and wiped my brow with a rag. "Thanks. I think it's my best ever."

Brigitte smiled. "The best possible time for it. By the way, Starborne …"

"Hm?" Trenco looked up. He'd been gazing at his slice of tarte, still half uneaten. I supposed he wanted to show his willpower by not finishing it, but doing so was clearly a burden.

"We may have been playing up the glorious majesty of baking a bit too strongly. What George has just finished making is pretty much the acme of the art, at least in terms of the regular menu, and I hope you enjoy his mille-feuilles when they're ready. But in the end, you know, it's just food. Ten minutes of pleasure, and a few hundred excess calories, no more. It matters to us personally because we've invested so much time and effort in learning how to do it. You know?"

Trenco grunted.

"But honestly," Brigitte continued, "it's not such a big deal as all that. Given the sugar-cane cuttings I hope to bring back home, we could provide sugar-solution ampules for people to carry around in case of emergency, and there'd be no need for pâtisserie shops. Probably it's the best thing to do in any event. It's just … we evolved on Earth to take pleasure in this kind of food. And I'm confident there's nothing demonic about it. All I really want is to share this pleasure with our people. Is that so very wrong?"

"Hmf."

"Pardon me," she said. "I shouldn't press you on the subject, as the trial isn't over yet."

At this point Jean finally returned.

"Geneviève," he said before any of us could greet him, "would you give me a minute? It's important."

"Of course."

Brigitte looked at me inquiringly as they headed for the door, but I shrugged, not having any more idea than her what he wanted to talk about. I was already turning back to Trenco when I realized something was happening.

Geneviève and Jean were standing stock still with the door open. They both took a step back in unison and a workman in a green jumpsuit entered after them. I realized two things at the same time: first, it was Jules from the Moulins Bourgeois, and second, he was holding a gun.

Chapter 8

Pardon the intrusion

Pardon the intrusion," he said, "mesdames, messieurs. But if you will please back up and stand against the far wall, no one will get hurt."

"Do what he says," said Geneviève. "This is the salaud Moreau from the DCRG. His people are traitors and assassins."

Moreau, formerly Jules, looked pained. "That business on the N3 was an accident. That damn fool analyst of yours decided to play the hero and he lost control of his car. All we wanted to do was ask Monier a few questions about—about *him*." He nodded at me.

"Oh? What about the assassin you sent after a civilian baking student?"

"The motorcyclist? He wasn't ours."

"He admitted it in hospital."

"I could admit I was President de Gaulle, and it wouldn't mean anything more than that. But *someone* in one of our groups must be a mole. DST or DCRG, or the assassin wouldn't have told that story. The whole Sûreté has been in an uproar for the last day because of that guy."

We'd all risen and started heading for the wall, Trenco only doing so after a nod from Brigitte. I noticed that Geneviève was angling for the end of our line where she would be closest to the counter on which she'd left her bag.

After we took our places, Geneviève said, "Well, one way or another you and your group are traitors. Because *we're* loyal, so who is it you're serving? The Russians? The Chinese?"

"We are loyal to France," said Moreau a bit prissily. "But not to the stupid isolationism of the gangster de Gaulle. We're for international cooperation. And so, Mademoiselle"—he nodded to Brigitte—"and Monsieur"—to Trenco—"if you would be so kind as to hand over the eggs I am reliably informed are in your possession I'll be happy to leave you to your baking. Because those items will lead not only to the removal of our current criminal leader, but also to closer ties with our allies."

"Oh," said Geneviève. "I understand now. It's the Americans, isn't it? You're selling your country out to the CIA. That's it, right?"

Moreau smiled. "They will provide assistance during the transition."

Geneviève sniffed. "I'm not that fond of de Gaulle myself. He really isn't much more than a thug, just as you say. But you know, he *was* elected president. And breaking our solemn treaty and working toward a coup … come on now. That's not playing the game, is it?"

Moreau shrugged. "I suppose we shall have to agree to disagree. But now I will collect the controllers and be on my way."

"I think not. *Don't move!*"

The door had opened while we were focused on Moreau, and another stranger entered. No, not a stranger, it was the agent from the cafe across from my place, now cleaned up and in a new suit. He too was holding a gun. Jules had spun halfway around before he realized he was covered, and froze in place when he saw he had no chance.

"Drozdov!" Trenco was furious. "How dare you show your face here! You bloody-handed demon!"

The agent Drozdov snickered. "You must forgive my deception, Monsieur alien. A little sin is worth the prize, however. And now it seems we will have two whole controllers, not just a twelfth share in one. No, no—" Trenco had made to approach him. "Don't move, Monsieur. All these lives hang in the balance. You would not wish to provoke me."

Trenco gritted his teeth, but resumed his place at the wall.

"Now then," said Drozdov to Moreau, "perhaps you will oblige me by very slowly placing your weapon on the floor. If you make a false move I will shoot you, and I tell you as a colonel of the first chief directorate of the KGB I will have no compunction about doing so."

"Not so fast."

With Drozdov's attention split between Moreau, who was still armed, and the truculent Trenco, Geneviève had taken the opportunity to retrieve her bag unnoticed and in one smooth motion she drew her own pistol, which she pointed at the Russian.

"Your turn to freeze," she said. "Both of you are under arrest, but if you move a muscle I too will be forced to shoot. Drozdov, is it? Put your pistol on the floor and slide it over here."

There was a terrible moment in which I saw both men, Drozdov and Moreau, were considering their chances. But neither of them wanted to make the first move, and neither of them had their guns on Geneviève.

Very slowly and carefully, Drozdov bent and placed his gun on the floor. He gave it a shove, and it skittered to our side of the room, stopping at Jean's feet.

"Now, Arkady Nikolaevich," the Russian growled. "Your time has come!"

Jean picked up the gun but didn't point it at anyone. He coughed and seemed desperately uncomfortable. "What I wanted to tell you, Geneviève … I'm not who you thought I was."

"Oh. Oh, Jean …" Now that Drozdov had been disarmed she had her gun trained on Moreau, but I could see her horror and dismay.

"What are you waiting for, fool?" Drozdov again.

Jean ejected the clip from the pistol and worked the slide to pump the bullet in the chamber out as well. He put the empty gun down on the counter and turned to face Geneviève, ignoring the Russian.

"I'd been trying to work my way up to telling you. I'm GRU deep cover. Not connected to this guy or his operation, but—"

Drozdov uttered something in Russian. It sounded bitter and heartfelt. Jean (Arkady?) turned back to him.

"Oh no, comrade," said Jean. "I don't think I'm a traitor at all. Don't you think it's better for the Soviet Union to uphold its honor by *not* breaking the most important treaty it has ever signed?"

"But the enemy acted first!" Drozdov switched back to French. "These creatures in the DCRG were going to seize the woman's controller. Our mole gave us a copy of the planning document. We had to preempt them. You see that, don't you? And then this naïf offered himself up to us, he actually presented himself at the embassy, so we could hardly turn him down. The DCRG and their CIA bosses would have laughed at their good fortune if we hadn't acted first."

Jean shrugged. "I suppose there's an argument to be made there. But you shouldn't have tried to assassinate my friend George. That was crossing a line."

Drozdov flushed. "Ah, yes. That was a mistake. I wouldn't have ordered it myself. SMERSH can get a little excitable at times, I admit. But we honestly thought he was MI-6 and that he'd stolen the woman's controller."

"Even so. How does that justify it? But I misspoke a moment ago. I should have said I *was* GRU deep cover. I just five minutes ago tendered my resignation with the military attaché at the Soviet embassy. Now I'm simply a poor homeless refugee seeking asylum. Well. And a diplôme de pâtisserie to boot if one happens to be forthcoming. So, I can't be turning a weapon on a law-enforcement officer in what I hope to be my new country. It wouldn't be right, you see. Not to mention she's my fiancée."

This silenced Drozdov for the moment as he had to pause to process the information. Moreau still had a gun in his hand, however, and from his body language I was increasingly worried he might try to use it despite Geneviève having the drop on him.

Just then the door opened for yet a third time. At this point I wouldn't have been surprised by a squad of marines much less another agent, but it was only Madame Dulaurier. She was enough of a distraction that Moreau felt this was his chance. He spun around, brought up his gun, and I heard the sound of a shot, deafeningly loud in the enclosed space of the kitchen.

I stared rather stupidly for a moment. Moreau's gun was on the floor in pieces, and his index finger was bent back at an unnatural angle. I glanced at Geneviève but she was recovering from the distraction of the door opening, and hadn't fired herself. Then I realized that Madame had a small portfolio case in one hand, but in the other she was holding her own pistol.

Moreau cursed, but froze again when he realized that two guns were now pointing his way. He turned red, then paled and clutched his hand and seemed on the verge of fainting. For a moment I almost felt sorry for him.

"I wouldn't move," said our professeur, "if I were you. Let's just sort this out, shall we?"

"Oh, no," said Geneviève. "Madame? *You're* an agent too? This I can't believe. It's … it's too much."

Madame Dulaurier smiled. "More of a freelancer. But you needn't fear, my dear comtesse. I really am a professeur de pâtisserie first. It happens I was in the Special Operations Executive during the war, however, and my former masters thought it prudent to pay a small retainer for me to keep an eye on things here."

"MI-6. I *knew* they'd have someone," said Geneviève. "I just guessed wrong about who it was. All that's wanting is for someone to turn out to be Chinese as well."

She squinted my way, but I could only shake my head. Then it occurred to me.

"This is terrible! I'm the only civilian in the room. What must you all have thought of me?"

Brigitte, Jean, and Geneviève all tried to speak up at once, but Madame Dulaurier silenced them just by opening her mouth. "I'd say he's the perfect model of a modern English pastry chef. Which brings us to an important point. The mille-feuilles must be cool by now. Where's the tea?"

I wound up splitting my pastries eight ways, because poor M. Moreau was in such a distraught combination of pain (even after Geneviève popped his dislocated finger back into the joint) and fear for his future I couldn't bear not to serve him too, while the KGB agent Drozdov became perfectly chummy when he realized that the American plot had been thwarted. "I have diplomatic immunity, anyway," he said. "I suppose it would have been better for the revolution to spread to other planets early, but so long as the imperialists don't win, my chiefs will no doubt be satisfied."

We had to wait a few minutes for Geneviève to make a series of calls to her director to apprise him of events. She clearly relieved Moreau's mind by telling him, "I can't promise anything, myself, but I expect the president and his ministers will prefer to keep everything quiet. Which means no prosecutions, of course. Perhaps it would be best to seek a future career outside of law enforcement, however."

Brigitte took the first bite of one of my mille-feuilles. I couldn't quite bear to try it myself. She cleaned off the excess crème from her mouth with her tongue and a moment later, speaking through a mouthful, said, "George! This is perfect! It's absolutely exquisite!"

Really I should have been more worried about Madame's opinion, or Trenco's, but a curious warmth seemed to suffuse my veins at her words. A tingle worked its way down my spine, and I found I couldn't say anything at all in response. But Brigitte caught my eye, and I felt she knew how gratified I was.

Trenco had remained quiet during all this confrontation and conversation, but I was happy to see that he had to restrain a certain eagerness to be served his half a pastry. Madame Dulaurier, however, carefully observed every side of the mille-feuille before shocking me by lifting the whole thing in her hand and taking a hearty bite. Crème pâtissière spurted out onto her plate, and she left some on her cheek for a good half minute while thoughtfully chewing and swallowing. It was only then that she patted away the residue with a serviette.

"I've always found it quite impossible to eat mille-feuilles neatly," she said. "So rather than embarrass myself with a knife and fork, I don't even try anymore. Shocking, I know."

A little hesitantly, Trenco followed her lead, making even more a mess than she had. The jam in Jean's financier might have been more purely sweet than the crème pâtissière or even my icing, but my overall achievement was the sweetest of the three pâtisserie products he'd tried, and I could see the combination of vanilla and chocolate along with the buttery puff-pastry was having a considerable impact, as he closed his eyes and leaned back while savoring the taste.

At this point a group of inspectors from the police judiciaire arrived to take Drozdov and Moreau into custody, the former showing his diplomatic corps get-out-of-jail-free card, the latter still trying to swallow his last bite of mille-feuille as his hands were cuffed.

"I'm under strict instructions from the minister of the interior," said the chief inspector, a big, portly fellow in late middle-age. "No questions to be asked and no evidence gathered. No formal questions, anyway. But really, inspector," he nodded to Geneviève, "the Sûreté in a shootout at the Cordon Blanc, of all places? This is bound to go down as a black mark."

"You're in the Sûreté now yourself, you know, Chief." The police judiciaire and the Sûreté had recently merged, much to the displeasure of both organizations.

The chief inspector snorted. "I'd rather have it that it is *you*, dear colleague, who are now in *my* Police Nationale. But I take your point. Let us say that at the Quai des Orfèvres we still feel a certain resentment toward the Rue de Saussaies."

Geneviève bowed stiffly and the police chief smiled at her. "But it seems that all is well here, however. Good work, inspector."

After that crowd departed, leaving us six behind, Geneviève blushed and lowered her voice to a whisper, though it was quite impossible that the chief inspector could hear her, "I … I had a crush on him when I was little."

Jean and I exchanged glances. "Should I grow a mustache too?" he asked. "I stand fast at dyeing my hair gray, however."

"You're not out of the woods, yet, Monsieur Môle," she said, and he grinned.

"I hear there's a fast track to citizenship for defectors. And for émigré husbands of French citizens, too. Then, too, I have a useful and marketable skill!"

Geneviève couldn't help smiling in response; their eyes met and they shared a rather charming moment together from which we all looked dutifully away.

After a decent pause, Madame Dulaurier unzipped her portfolio case and produced some parchment squares.

"Now that the charming domestic exchange has concluded, it's my pleasure to announce that all three of you have graduated the Institut. Mention Très Bien, no less. Rarely have I seen such uniform dedication from any group of three students."

She handed out the certificates in turn, shook each of our hands, and kissed us each on both cheeks.

"Mademoiselle … Birgud. Monsieur … Arkady Nikolaevich Vasiliev. And Monsieur George … well. I suppose your name really *is* Drake. How strange! Well. I shall follow your careers with *considerable* interest. Good luck to you all. Please excuse me; I have a few kitchens left to … pacify."

Five of us were left, now. Brigitte addressed Trenco.

"Well, Starborne, I'm sorry that our baking trial had to be so … fraught. I assure you this isn't the usual thing. But what do you think? Is pâtisserie demonic? Or divine?"

The alien visitor coughed. "Ah … you said a while back that we … that we Templars believe things that are contrary to the facts. Perhaps it would be better to say we believe things for which facts are unavailable. That we have faith. It would be worse than foolish to deny one's own senses. Blasphemous, even. But fortunately, it seems I have compressed a great deal of experience into just a few days. So. This is my judgment.

"Earth is a desperately backwards world. The planet and its people are both in dire need of grace and enlightenment. However … horrifying as my time here has been in some respects, I must modify my initial opinion. I have seen no trace of demonic influence as yet. There may well be some such … contamination, as scripture indicates, but neither you people, nor your food are … infernal. As such …"

He raised his hand and for a moment I saw that curious rainbow gleam again.

"As such, I rescind my ban. Explorer Birgud, you are free to return to Blossom. I only beg that you take care with such foreign introductions as you choose to attempt. Not all change is for the best."

Brigitte performed an intricate and prolonged gesture, something like a minute-long sequence of Buddhist mudras, ending in a deep bow.

"You see, I remember my childhood devotions after all. But I'm in your debt, Starborne, and more than that, I'm very pleased that we are no longer opponents. At least not in the same sense as earlier today."

Geneviève exhaled noisily. "Well. This is a relief. Brigitte, I'd love to remain, but I have department chiefs and ministers to placate, not to mention a high-ranking defector to process, and I'm afraid I will just have to submit to these officious demands for the rest of the day. But you—you won't go home immediately, will you? You'll let me call on you later on?"

"Of course," said Brigitte. "How could I be so rude, to such a close friend! We four—we five, if the Starborne wishes—shall certainly have time for another dinner, at least."

Chapter 9

A cosmic flowering

Only three of us were left. Of course I was happy with how things had turned out, but desperately unhappy at the same time, because I still hadn't had a chance to communicate anything I wanted to Brigitte, and even now had no idea what I was supposed to do. So, I stood there miserable and silent for what seemed like an eternity before she turned to me.

"My dear George," she said. "What can I say to you? Thank you is insufficient. Especially when—when I have yet to complete my mission. There's no help for it, I'm afraid. I must return to Blossom with my seeds and my cuttings and my recipes, not just for the good of my own people, but for the good of Earth as well. Too much violence has already occurred, and it would be terrible of me to stay on here, no matter how much I want to. No matter how much I want to remain with you."

"Oh," I said, "I quite understand—" but then her last words struck home. I hadn't been expecting that, not even a little bit, and it stunned me speechless.

She smiled and put a hand on my cheek; I wasn't sure whether to withdraw or take her into my arms, so I did nothing. As usual.

She said, "I'm afraid there may be some delay before I can return to Earth. When I do, it will be incognito, too; I've had enough of this spy stuff to last me a lifetime. But my dear, if you would be willing to wait a while, I promise to return."

Trenco coughed. I'd forgotten he was there. "Er. Pardon me. I realize I'm intruding."

"Yes?" Brigitte withdrew her hand (it felt like a tragic loss) and turned to him with a somewhat apprehensive look on her face.

"It occurs to me that not all my … my Templar peers will necessarily be convinced by my testimony, incomplete as it currently is. If the Earthling is willing, I think in his person he might convey a more convincing report of this world …"

"Wait," said Brigitte. "You'd do that for us?"

Trenco handed me a warm gray ovoid, shimmering with rainbow patterns. "I expect I'll require at least a year here to complete my investigation. I understand that the pâtisserie menu has quite a number of entries I haven't yet sampled … But that's neither here nor there. With no official presence, and without a controller of my own, I hope I won't be too much of a lure for violence."

My state of shocked amazement continued, redoubled. I barely had the presence of mind not to drop the controller.

"Oh! Oh, George! But—This is too much, isn't it? I couldn't possibly expect—"

"I'll do it," I told her. "Are you crazy? How could I not? I just need to tell my parents … That's all right, isn't it? Telling them?"

"Of course! But—"

For once I managed to act on my own. I put my hand up against her cheek in turn. Her eyes widened, she put her hand over mine and—

Hand in hand, wearing suits of living light, the stars rushed by us, faster and faster, a rising chord sounding in our ears, rocketing through a tunnel of light, a rainbow brilliance gleaming all around us, and at last, a cosmic flowering of transcendence and glory …

A green world zoomed into view against a dark background, growing larger and brighter as we rushed towards it, passing through blue skies and white clouds to alight on a pedestal on the roof of a tower. We were in a small but lovely city densely planted with trees like giant cycads showing enormous fanlike sprays of leaves. Brigitte took me in her arms and I took her in mine and when we broke from the kiss she said, "Welcome to Blossom."

END

Acknowledgements

Thanks to all my friends and colleagues in my writing groups, including everyone at Codex, my Viable Paradise cohort, the members of Seventh Prime, and my Elementals critique group. Your critiques and support have been enormously helpful and your friendship even more valuable.

About the Author

Laurence Raphael Brothers is a writer and a technologist. He has published over 50 short stories in such magazines as *Nature*, *PodCastle*, and *The New Haven Review*.

For the latest news, check his website at https://laurencebrothers.com or follow him on Bluesky at @lrb.bsky.social. Pronouns: he/him.

MORE FROM BRIGIDS GATE PRESS

FALLEN DESTINY

Yolanda Sfetsos

Destiny isn't human and she has the horns to prove it. She's also damned good at blending into the human world.

That, along with her powers, has helped her forge a career out of locating **supernatural beings** and objects.

Got **demon** troubles? Need a mystical artifact found? Destiny's the one for the job.

All goes well for her until the day she's hired by a mysterious **nun**, and for the first time, Destiny's stumped.

How exactly does a demon hired by a nun find an **angel**?

THE WOLF AND THE FAVOUR

Catherine McCarthy

Ten-year-old Hannah has Down syndrome and oodles of courage, but should she trust the alluring tree creature who smells of Mamma's perfume or the blue-eyed wolf who warns her not to enter the woods under any circumstance?

The Wolf and the Favour is a tale of love, trust, and courage. A tale that champions the neurodivergent voice and proves the true power of a person's strength lies within themselves.

Dissonance of Bird Song

Alexandra Beaumont

In the storm-riven wilds of ancient Cornwall the sea's whisper will charm us all.

Dissonance of Bird Song is the folkloric-fantasy tale of Eseld, a song-weaver fleeing her home to cure the sacred birds of her people and save her sister. Locked between the lies of land-dwellers and the snare of an ancient sea queen, Eseld must fight to find her own path. Amidst a storm of betrayal and heartbreak, what will Eseld sacrifice to save the ones she loves?

Readers who enjoyed Lucy Hounsom's *Sistersong*, Naomi Novik's *Uprooted*, and Natasha Bowen's *Skin of the Sea* will love *Dissonance of Bird Song*.

THE HIDING

Alethea Lyons

Arcane archivist Harper has always been plagued by dreams of grotesque creatures and bloody deaths. When she bumps into a ghostwalker in the Shambles and has a visceral experience of his execution, she knows it's a foretelling. Yet fear of the Queen's Guard stops her speaking out. When her vision indeed comes true, the unusual markings on the ghostwalker's corpse, combined with his neatly excised vocal cords, send a ripple of terror through York.

The witch hunt is on. As the body count rises, Harper knows her magic is the only way to find the killer – if she can avoid being hanged as a witch. To protect both human and supernatural, Harper walks the thin line between their worlds. She and her demonhunter foster-sister form a multi-faith team with a forensic scientist, a spirit Harper accidentally summoned, and a techno-witch, to catch the killer before more people die.

Visit our website at: www.brigidsgatepress.com